Her own screams echoed in her ears.

Help me, somebody help me get my sister. The flames rose around them in angry tongues, unforgiving, unrelenting.

Jerking back to the present, Ivy tried again to roll over. A collage of dark smoke and gray shadows danced in her vision. She had to reach the radio in her pocket, but she couldn't move, couldn't breathe. The space grew hotter with every passing second. She knew it, she could feel it, the junk all around her inching closer and closer to ignition.

It would be simultaneous.

And deadly.

Flashover.

Again, Ivy struggled to wriggle loose, to free herself from the enormous weight that smothered her. Pain coursed through her head and shoulder. Somewhere from the vicinity of her pocket, she heard a shrill alarm sound on her radio. Then there was nothing but heat as the blackness enveloped her.

Books by Dana Mentink

Love Inspired Suspense

Killer Cargo
Flashover

DANA MENTINK

Dana Mentink lives in California with her family. Dana and her husband met doing a dinner theater production of *The Velveteen Rabbit*. In college, she competed in national speech and debate tournaments. Besides writing novels, Dana taste tests for the National Food Lab and freelances for a local newspaper. Dana loves feedback from her readers. Contact her at www.danamentink.com.

FLASHOVER

DANA MENTINK

Steeple
Hill®

Published by Steeple Hill Books™

STEEPLE HILL BOOKS

Steeple
Hill®

Recycling programs
for this product may
not exist in your area.

ISBN-13: 978-0-373-44324-6
ISBN-10:   0-373-44324-2

FLASHOVER

www.SteepleHill.com

Printed in U.S.A.

Therefore as God's chosen people, holy and dearly loved, clothe yourselves with compassion, kindness, humility, gentleness and patience. Bear with each other and forgive whatever grievances you may have against one another. Forgive as the Lord forgave you. And over all these virtues put on love, which binds them all together in perfect unity.
—*Colossians* 3:12–14

To the everyday heroes who silently strive to lift others up, not for their own glory, but for His.

ONE

Black smoke swelled in graceful scallops as it climbed in a thick column against the midday sun, mirroring the excitement that rose in her gut. Two-story structure fire, flames showing. Perfect.

Ivy could see the thrill in Jeff's face, too, accentuated by the strobing lights of the fire truck. "Finally, some action. My wife says I've been moping around because things have been so quiet. She offered to go out and set something on fire for me."

She laughed, tucking her razor-cut bob of sandy hair behind her ears as they both hopped down from the truck and jogged with their captain to meet Battalion Chief Adrienne Strong, who was already barking orders to the guys on the first engine. She looked small under her helmet and turnouts, but her brown eyes shone fiercely beneath a fringe of hair.

"Got a report of a victim trapped inside." She stabbed a finger at a member of the crowd that was massing on the sidewalk. "A witness says he saw the owner enter the building an hour ago. He's short, a little nuts, goes by the name of Cyril. Nobody saw him come out."

Why did the name Cyril ring a bell? Ivy looked closely at the structure, which now had flames flickering through the upstairs windows. She could see outlines of boxes and furniture, stacked floor to ceiling. If the view was any indication, there would be only a small trail of usable space weaving throughout all the garbage. She sighed. "Oh, man. It looks like a Habitrail. He's got enough junk to start his own flea market."

She buckled on the ax belt, waiting for the captain to turn off the utilities. Her muscles tensed in anticipation, fingers itching to put on the mask and get inside. Instinctively she looked around for Antonio, larger than life in his turnouts. Then she remembered. *Antonio moved on, Ivy. You better do the same.*

When the captain gave the thumbs-up, Ivy started toward the structure.

"Wait, Beria." Strong talked again into the radio. "This is going to be ugly with all that garbage in there. Let's get it ventilated first. Help them work the front door. Jeff, see if you can get any of those witnesses to confirm we have a victim in there."

Ivy joined the two firefighters who were attacking the front door with a pry tool. The door was heavy oak, and though they heaved with all their strength, the wood gave up only reluctantly. They alternately pushed the bar and kicked at the wood with their booted feet until the wood gave with a final groan. Clouds of blackness surged out, forcing them back.

She returned to the chief in time to hear Jeff's report.

"No one can corroborate the story. The owner is apparently some kind of eccentric."

"No kidding," Ivy muttered.

Jeff raised his voice to be heard over the hum of the pumper and the whoosh of water thundering through the hose. "His schedule is erratic. No one saw him come out, but they weren't looking, either."

They watched as a firefighter, barely visible except for the flash of the fluorescent tape on his turnouts, moved past them at the nozzle end of the two-hundred-foot hose, his captain behind, sweat already coating their faces under the breathing apparatus. Ducking as low as they could manage, the two made entry.

Ivy looked past them as she and Jeff pulled on their own masks and picked their way to the door to peer inside. As she did so, she thought she saw movement from the trees next to the house. It was a glimpse really, a split-second look, but she could have sworn she saw Moe, her neighbor at the apartment complex. But what would he be doing here?

She jogged over. It was Moe, and he was shivering. "What's wrong?"

"Cyril," he said, pointing to the house then bounding away. Who was Cyril?

She refocused her attention on the house. The place was indeed a maze of junk, piled against all the walls and in towering columns in the foyer and front rooms. She strained her eyes to get a glimpse of a human form but blackness obscured everything.

Strong's radio crackled to life and she called to them. "Engine Twenty-Five is en route from a spill in Pine Grove. Their ETA is five minutes. Beria and Jones, you wait. I'm going to pull the other crew in another minute."

Ivy huffed as they trotted back. Wait? What if this Cyril guy was inside? What if he was trapped, shouting for help, and she was out here, useless? A horrifying memory fought through her control. She swallowed hard and shoved it down. "Let us go in, Chief. The victim could be in there." Ivy looked at the flames licking at the windows and her stomach clenched. "We can do a quick assessment and get out."

She shook her head. "Wait until we can get it ventilated. Twenty-Five is less than four minutes out." Frustration was painted on the chief's face, probably the consequence of being a small fire department with older equipment and only two stations to provide personnel. Her struggle was clear in the lines on her forehead and around her mouth. Potential victim versus potential injury to her people.

Antonio would have made his case by now. Ivy pressed her advantage. "In four more minutes he could be dead." She couldn't let that happen, especially if the man inside was possibly a friend of Moe.

The chief clenched her jaw muscles. "No, Beria."

Ivy knew Strong had seen many fatalities in her career from traffic accidents to drownings, but being unable to save a victim from burning to death was unthinkable, for both of them. "It would just be a quick sweep, then we're out of there."

Strong looked from Ivy to Jeff and exhaled. "Okay. One

sweep and you're out." She grabbed the sleeve of Jeff's turnout coat as he pulled on his breathing apparatus. "If anything feels bad, you pull the plug. You got it?"

He nodded. They ran toward the acrid swirl of black.

Ivy could feel the chief's anxious eyes following them. Strong would be confirming the crew outside who would stand ready to pull them out if they'd need it. The thought comforted her as they pushed their way onto the ground floor. The carpet was spongy underfoot, already saturated with water. They both instinctively bent over, staying closer to the clean air. Heat pushed through their heavy protective layers.

It took only a moment to weave their way around the junk piles on the ground floor. No victims. Jeff jerked a thumb upward. Ivy nodded. The upper floor was where they were most likely to find anyone, alive or dead.

They followed the hose line up the stairs and found the two firefighters struggling to keep up with the flames. Cardboard boxes and rolls of carpet provided an ample supply of fuel for the hungry fire. The man at the nozzle end was trying to aim for the base of the fire, which thundered from an open bedroom doorway.

She prayed for the boom of a ladder hitting the side of the house that would announce the guys on Engine Twenty-Five had made it to the roof to ventilate. The hole they cut would suck all the black smoke out like a vacuum and restore visibility in minutes. But there wasn't time to sit around hoping. She and Jeff headed through a maze of debris toward the back bedrooms.

The heat was intense. Sweat poured down her face under the mask and soaked through the Nomex hood. She could feel the molten temperature through the thick gloves as she pushed her way by stacks of piled furniture.

Jeff was a few yards ahead. He'd found a locked door, and though the handle turned, it wouldn't open. He tried to force it with the pry bar.

"It's unlocked," he yelled above the noise. "But I can't budge it."

Both of them threw their combined weight at the door and it finally opened.

Flames erupted through the opening, driving them back. The room was fully engulfed.

Jeff did a cutting motion across his throat. "We're out of here, Ivy. It's gonna go up any minute." He grabbed the radio from his pocket and the battalion chief officially ordered them all to pull out. Ahead in the hallway she could see the two hosemen inching back down the stairs.

Jeff turned and followed them, his sturdy form disappearing after a few steps in the dark haze.

Ivy made to follow him when she noticed the door at the end of the hall. It had to open onto a bedroom. After a moment's hesitation she got on her hands and knees and crawled toward it. The man might be inside, calling out, his voice too weak to be heard over the cacophony. The heat intensified with each foot of floor she crossed. Her helmet felt like a vise, pressing in around her face, squeezing the breath out of her. She should follow Jeff, get out before the place went up.

But what if there was a life on the other side of that door?

A life that she was meant to save?

She moved as fast as she could toward the threshold, following the narrow strip of space that wound through the junk. Inches away, she reached out a hand to push the door open. The fingers of her gloves barely grazed the painted wood when the towering pile shuddered crazily and collapsed on top of her.

Metal pipes and crates filled with something heavy crashed down. Mountains of boxes and furniture continued to rain on top of her. The crash was deafening as she was buried in the avalanche. Something struck her head, and a knifing pain shot through her temple.

She lay on her back struggling to turn over, but the heavy debris and the weight of her air tanks immobilized her. Her face shield was fogged with moisture and soot. A collage of dark smoke and gray shadows danced in her vision. She had to reach the radio in her pocket, but she couldn't move, couldn't breathe.

The room closed in around her as she fought against the panic. Her mind spun into the past. Glimmers of memory shot through her and she could see, painted in perfect detail, her sister's face, trapped behind the glass.

She strained every muscle, every sinew to reach out and free her. *Sadie, Sadie.* Her own screams from long ago echoed in her ears. *Help me, somebody help me get my sister.* The flames rose around them in angry tongues, unforgiving, unrelenting.

Jerked back into the present, Ivy tried again to roll over. The space grew hotter with every passing second. She knew it, she could feel it, the junk all around her inching closer and closer to ignition.

It would be simultaneous.

And deadly.

Flashover.

Again she struggled to wriggle loose, to free herself from the enormous weight that smothered her. Pain coursed through her head and shoulder. Every minuscule movement caused the pile to shudder and close in around her, filling in the spaces like sand poured into a jar. It was no use. She didn't have the strength. The burden was too much to bear.

Somewhere from the vicinity of her pocket, she heard a shrill alarm sound. The shriek cut through everything else, filling the space, making her ears pulse with pain. Then there was nothing but heat as she gave herself up to the blackness that enveloped her body and soul.

Nick nestled himself into the crowd. All eyes were turned to the brilliant orange flames. He didn't mind the acrid tang of smoke. It reminded him of back home, burning leaves in the fall. A photographer jostled his way to the front, camera pointed at the blaze. Nick was careful to step out of the way, admiring the camera as he did so. The irony was not lost on him. The paper would feature the fire in glorious detail while the artist would remain invisible just behind the photographer's left elbow.

He itched to take a picture, too, with the elite camera he'd seen in a magazine. A Horseman, two lenses sharing a single shutter at lightning speed. It was not digital, of course, but he preferred it that way, relishing the anticipation that came as he waited for the film to develop. Waiting was a skill, a talent so many people lacked.

Nick pondered the conversation he'd observed between the woman firefighter and the strange guy he knew to be Cyril's friend. He'd heard that the fellow's name was Moe. Did Moe know anything incriminating? Anything he might have passed along to the firefighter? It bore consideration, but for now, Nick allowed himself to enjoy the fiery spectacle unfolding before him.

"Did you hear that?" a cadaverous old woman next to him hissed. "They said there's a firefighter trapped inside."

She clutched his arm as a pane of glass shattered on the upper floor. He patted her bony fingers. "It's incredible, all right."

He watched a spark, brilliant as a comet, explode from the roof and paint a luminous arc across the smoky sky. *Definitely front-page material,* he thought with satisfaction.

TWO

Tim Carnelli fought to keep the truck's speed under control.
Ivy.

Her name echoed in his mind and danced circles around his brain.

He knew before he heard the name. He knew when the battalion chief's voice came over the radio, pitched high against adrenaline and the sound of a working fire. Firefighter down.

"God help her," he whispered as he tore down the main road through a thickening haze of smoke. "Help her to hang on."

If he had more time to process, the irony would be palpable. Was it just last night he'd decided to move on? Even looking up Marcie's number to give her a call? Forget about Ivy, he'd told himself. You were a fool to think she'd open her heart to you after Antonio. She might never trust anyone again, especially God.

He clenched the steering wheel so hard his fingers cramped up. Not now. It wasn't time to dredge up past history.

Even so, an image rose in his mind. Ivy's short hair blowing in the breeze, green eyes alight with laughter as they rode mountain bikes together in the pre-Antonio days.

Ivy.

His heart thundered in his chest as the radio crackled to life again.
Life flight.

The dispatcher calmly repeated the message and confirmed. They were calling for the helicopter.

He wasn't a firefighter, but everyone connected to the business knew what it meant when they called for a helicopter.

And it wasn't good.

Strange sensations flooded Ivy's senses. She felt the bump of the gurney as she was rolled along, the shouted commands of firefighters amped on adrenaline, and then inexplicably, Tim was there. When had he arrived at the fire scene? He must have heard the call go out on the radio.

She wanted to tell him she was okay, to ease the terror written on his usually smiling face, but her mouth would not cooperate. He squeezed her arm with his strong fingers.

"It's okay, Ivy. You're going to make it through this."

She felt her own fear ease slightly. She tried to hold his hand, but he was abruptly pulled away. He mouthed something she couldn't hear as she was loaded onto a helicopter. The chopper blades cut through the air with rhythmic whopping sounds.

A familiar voice spoke up over the noise. Ivy's eyes were closed, but she knew it was her cousin, Mitch. She could smell his cologne through the oxygen mask, over the odor of antiseptic and bandages the medics had applied. She was comforted knowing Mitch was the on-duty flight nurse. He was the best.

"Come on, V. Open up those green eyes. You can do it. Imagine we're back in the country and I'm about to whip you at hide-and-seek. You never won once in our entire childhood, remember? And then there's pinball. I can beat you with one hand tied behind my back. What do you say to that?"

Mitch Luzan's face swam into view. Curly black hair, thick eyebrows, sardonic smile on his chubby face. Even though she was immobilized except for her arms, strapped from head to toe to a backboard, the sight of him brought her comfort.

"That's 'cuz you cheat." Her voice came out as a croak, muffled by the mask.

"Well, that's better." He used a small light to check her pupils. "Imagine getting a call to come and transport a victim and finding out it's you. And to think I tried to get out of this shift." He shook his head and checked her IV. "That was pretty dumb, letting yourself get buried. I thought they trained you hotshots how to prevent stuff like that. What happened to the big bad invincible Beria?"

She tried to answer but succumbed instead to a coughing fit. Pulling off the mask, she waved away his hands. "What's broken?" she finally managed.

"Well, if I had to make a diagnosis right now I'd say we're looking at collarbone and shoulder damage, a concussion, possible internal stuff and a burn or two."

She grimaced at the list. "I'm fine. Just banged up."

He leaned over to put on his helmet for the landing and zipped the jumpsuit, which strained to cover his stomach. "Tell you what, V. How about you let me be the flight nurse, because I am an excellent one after all, and you just work on doing the patient thing for a while? That will be a challenge for you, I know, Miss I Gotta Be in Charge of Everything." He began to radio information to the hospital.

There was an edge to his voice. She looked closer and noticed dark shadows under his eyes. She hadn't seen him for months even though they lived only two towns apart. He was closer to her than her brother, in some ways, until recently.

Ivy closed her eyes and sighed. She was too tired to ask where he'd been the past few months, in too much pain to wonder about the haggard cast to his face.

She tried to replay the accident but could only get to the point when her personal distress indicator went off. The guys must have pulled her out before the place went up. Or maybe they'd gotten the roof ventilated and knocked down the fire. Not knowing the details was killing her.

She strained her eyes to find Mitch and pump him for info, but he was busy prepping the equipment that would follow her into the hospital. As the helicopter roared in for a landing, she let herself sink back into darkness.

People moved in and out of her consciousness. Dressed in white or green scrubs, they checked every detail, cleaned every abrasion and treated her with tender care in spite of her exclamations of pain. Vaguely she was aware of a doctor peeling off his gloves and announcing that he would brief her colleagues waiting in the hallway. That brought her around.

She opened her eyes to find her shoulder strapped firmly to her body. When she tried to sit up, a lancing pain drove her back to the pillow. A shower of sparks danced across her vision. Gingerly she felt the bandage stuck to her forehead and another taped over the burn on her neck.

Battalion Chief Strong appeared, Jeff next to her. They were both sooty, tired, their faces lined with worry, turnouts streaked with black.

Jeff's smile was huge as he grabbed her hand. "Man, Ivy. You scared me. I thought you were done for. That place was cooking."

She tried to return the smile. "Did you pull me out?"

He nodded. "Eventually. I didn't know you were gone until your alarm sounded as I headed out the front door. I went back in and the rescue crew followed me. We found you under a pile of junk. Took all three of us to get the stuff off you, and I was nearly out of air by that time." His expression changed. "What happened anyway? I thought you were right behind me. I told you we were leaving. Didn't you hear me?"

She coughed. "I stopped to check the last door."

He frowned. "Ivy…"

Chief Strong touched his arm. "Jeff, go get me some water, will you? I feel like I swallowed a sock."

Jeff gave Ivy a nervous look and squeezed her hand before he left. "I'll tell the rest of the guys you're okay."

Strong waited until he was gone before she sat heavily in a chair. Her hair was plastered against her head where her helmet had weighted it down. She smelled of smoke. "I'm glad you're going to be okay."

Ivy saw the warring emotions on the woman's face and knew there was more coming. "Thanks, Chief. Was anybody else hurt?"

She pursed her lips. "No, and that's a lucky thing, isn't it?"

Ivy swallowed. "Sure."

"Did it occur to you when you disobeyed my orders to evacuate that you were being reckless and stupid?"

Ivy bridled. "I was doing my job. I didn't hang out in there to have a party or anything."

The brown eyes flashed. "You were doing what you decided your job was at that moment. I gave you a direct order, and last I checked, I outrank you. You risked the lives of the people who dragged your behind out of there and you had absolutely no right to do that."

Her cheeks felt hot. "There could have been someone inside. Did you find anyone?"

"No. The house was empty."

Ivy's stomach clenched at the thought. It had all been for nothing. They'd gone back in for her. What would she have done if one of them hadn't made it out? Because of her, all because of her.

They both sat in silence for a minute. Strong sighed deeply. "This isn't the time to get into it. We'll talk when you've recovered. Doc says you're out at least eight weeks before he'll reevaluate you."

"Eight weeks? Uh-uh. I'll be back before then. There's no way I'm staying out two months."

Strong got to her feet. Her tone masked a current of fury. "Ivy, you will stay out until that doctor gives me a written note telling me you are one hundred percent mended. Then you and I will have a long debriefing session about this fire before I let you back on my crew." She walked to the door and turned. "Thank goodness you're okay, Ivy. I would sure hate to be the one who had to tell your mother that you weren't. She's outside. I'll send her in."

Her mother.

The thought hit her like a slap. It wasn't the first time she wondered how her mother felt about her chosen profession, especially after what happened to Sadie. She'd never said a word to discourage Ivy's career choice, as much as it pained her. It must have been awful for her mother to get a call that her surviving daughter was caught in a fire.

Guilt gave way to another emotion. An anger swelled up inside her and spilled out.

Two months away from the station? Maybe more than that if things didn't heal right. She punched her good hand into the blankets. "Well, God? What are you doing up there? You are supposed to take care of your children," she hissed at the ceiling. "Look what happened to me. And what about Sadie? Haven't we had enough in this family? You're nothing like a father."

She quickly wiped the tears away at the sight of her mother barreling through the door. Juana Beria took one look at her and burst into hysterical sobs, tears running down her plump brown cheeks.

"Oh, Mama. Please don't cry. Anything but that."

Her mother's tears continued, unchecked. "When I think… When I imagine…"

Ivy closed her eyes. "Please, Mama. Don't."

It was messy, emotional, and the whole situation left Ivy completely exhausted.

"I brought you some clothes. The doctor says you'll be here for a few days. I'll go to your apartment and get you some more things, a nightgown and some books to read. I'll bring them first thing in the morning after you've rested," Juana Beria said, her round face still damp with tears. She looked to her son, who had joined them. "Roddy, you'll take me, won't you?" Though she had a license, Juana refused to drive anywhere since her husband had passed away five years prior.

Rodrigo, Ivy's brother, patted his mother's hand. "Sure, Mama, sure. I'll pick you up in the morning. We can bring her stuff over and then I'll take you home. Let's go." He shot Ivy a look of aggravation that made her smile. Anything that upset Mama was something to be avoided at all costs, and Ivy had done her share. With Ivy laid up, Roddy would shoulder the emotional burden of the latest family drama for sure.

She'd owe him, and he'd definitely collect on the debt. When the room was empty, she tried to sleep. The pain in her shoulder wouldn't let her. She wished she could take a shower and wash away the acrid smell that clung to her hair and skin.

A small tap sounded on the door. The tall, brown-haired man

stood hesitantly, his wide shoulders filling the doorway. Tim poked his head in. "Hey, Ivy? Are you awake?"

She sighed, feeling like smiling for the first time since she'd entered that burning building. "Hi, Tim. Come on in. Has the Beria family train departed yet?"

He laughed softly. "Yes, I think so. It's just me at the moment."

"Good, someone rational to talk to. Come sit down. I think I remember seeing you at the fire scene, or did I dream that?"

"No dream, it really was me. I heard the call on the scanner so I broke some land-speed records and hightailed it over. Got there just as they were pulling you out. I don't mind telling you I never want to see that again."

He settled his long frame into a chair and she held out a hand for his. They'd been friends for years, since before she went into the academy. *Maybe that's why we get along so well,* she thought. He wasn't part of that intense firefighter brotherhood; he had his own perspective on things. He wasn't your typical hero type, either. No, that was Antonio all the way. Thinking about Antonio made her cringe with humiliation.

Tim squeezed her fingers. "Are you okay? In much pain?"

The floodgates opened. She began to cry rivers of hot tears. "My shoulder hurts and I'm going to be out two months. Strong is really mad at me, too."

His brow crinkled. "Why?"

She took the tissue he offered. "I disobeyed orders and stayed in the house."

He was silent for a moment. "Oh, I see."

"You're not surprised, are you?"

"You do have a tendency to throw caution to the wind, Ivy." Then he said what she most needed to hear. "It will be okay. You'll heal and you'll go back to doing what you love."

She turned her tearstained face to his. The sunlight framed him, the asymmetrical smile and messy thatch of hair, outlining his strong chin. "Promise?"

He stroked her hand. "I promise. And I'll even help you work on throwing ladders to get back in shape."

She laughed. He was the most dismal failure at throwing ladders she'd ever seen. Stronger than she was, but not very coordinated. Ironic, since he was a gifted athlete. She often told him it was a good thing for public safety that he'd avoided fire suppression, instead becoming the fire district's computer guru. He was a willing helper, though. As long as he didn't start up his God talk, they got along great.

"Did you see Mitch? He brought me in."

Tim nodded. "Yeah. I was supposed to help him with some software stuff tonight but he said he's coming back here when he's off to check on you."

"He looked kinda funny in the chopper."

Tim looked away. "Funny? In what way?"

They were interrupted when the nurse came in to check her bandages and inform them it was time to take her for a CAT scan.

Tim stood and bumped into a rolling cart in the process. "Well, I'll just get moving then. Call me if you need anything, Ivy. I'm really glad you're okay. I'll pray for you."

She almost told him not to bother, but he'd already gone.

She watched the clock and dozed on and off until almost eight, when Mitch arrived with a huge bouquet of daisies in hand. "Hey, V. How is the patient?"

"I'm okay." She eyed his silk shirt and black jeans. "You didn't have to get all dressed up for me."

He dropped a kiss on her forehead. "I didn't. Actually I've got another thing tonight."

"A girl?" She was hopeful. He'd been so lonely since his long-term girlfriend left him for an anesthesiologist. He could use someone to talk to and share his need for adventure.

He handed her the flowers and settled into the chair. "Nothing too wild. A college friend of mine is passing through and we're getting a bite to eat. Charlie's coming along."

Charlie Gregor was the chopper pilot who flew the helicopter for Mitch's crew. She fingered the white petals. "That's good. Thanks for the flowers."

"You're welcome. Doc says he expects a full recovery."

"In *two months*. What am I supposed to do for two months?"

He smiled. "Here's an idea. Take a vacation, like normal people do. Relax, learn to knit or something."

"I'm not a good relaxer."

"Don't I know it. Give it a try, it might grow on you."

"I'd rather follow your book of rules. You're always up to something fun."

"Not all of us eat, sleep and breathe our jobs, V." A beep sounded from his PDA. He checked the screen. "That's my wake-up call. Time for me to split. I'll come back and see you soon. Try not to drive your nurses crazy."

"I might not be here when you come back. Maybe I'll check out tonight."

"Not for a few days, I think."

"Couldn't you talk to the doctor? Tell him…"

"No way, cousin. Lie there and take your healing like a grown-up." He stood and stretched his stocky arms. "Oh, I talked to Doug. He says it's going to be hard to prove."

Doug was the department's fire marshal. "What is?"

His eyes widened. "Didn't they tell you? I figured the chief would have let you know."

"She isn't even speaking to me right now." She frowned. "Tell me what?"

"The fire wasn't an accident. Looks like you've got an arsonist on the loose."

Nick hesitated only a moment before he knocked on the door. "There is a complication."

His boss frowned slightly. "Tell me."

"He got out."

"Are you sure?"

"Yes. I made it look like an accident as you suggested. He refused to tell me where he'd put it. After he was unconscious, I used a candle and waited until it lit the place. If it was anywhere in there, it's ashes now. The problem is fixed." He stood his ground, flinching slightly at the frown that grew on the other man's face.

"But there is the matter of Cyril's friend. It's possible Cyril passed on my merchandise to the man and he told the firefighter, isn't it?"

Nick nodded. "It crossed my mind. Should I take care of them?"

His boss rolled his eyes in thought. "For now, concentrate on finding Cyril and do what is necessary to find out if the girl knows anything. Don't kill her yet. It will draw too much attention."

Nick frowned. Finesse was not his strong suit. "What should I do if I find out the girl really does know? Or Moe?"

A slight smile crossed the boss's face. "If necessary, I'm sure you will prove resourceful enough to handle it."

Nick returned the smile and closed the door behind him as he left.

THREE

Ivy endured the remainder of the evening with bad TV, worse food and people trailing in and out feeling sorry for her. What's more, she began to feel sorry for herself.

"I went into that building, risked my life and my career for nothing. No victim, no rescue, and come to find out it's arson." Probably some guy trying to collect on the insurance, though what a junk hole like that could be worth was beyond her. The futility of the whole thing pained her.

When the doctor came in to see her in the early morning, she pounced. "I want to go home."

He looked over the top of his glasses. "A few more tests, I think. A day or two to rest."

"No. I want to get out of here now."

He sighed. "I'm not going to tie you up and keep you here, Ms. Beria. It's your health. If you want to go, go, but it's against my advice. Come back on Tuesday for a recheck of those burns. Keep your shoulder immobilized and stay out of trouble."

"Right." She grabbed the hospital phone and dialed Tim's number.

"I'm going home today. Can you give me a ride?" After a quick call to her mother to fill her in, Ivy pulled on her clothes.

Tim watched with an amused grin as a nurse pushed a mortified Ivy in a wheelchair out to the curb. He opened the passenger-side door for her.

She dove out of the wheelchair before it stopped rolling and hopped into the truck, buckling up gingerly around her injured shoulder. "Thanks for taking me home."

"You're welcome, but I'm still not sure it's a good idea. Your mother has another plan." He was careful to keep his eyes on the road as they continued on.

She stared. "What are you talking about?"

"Your mom called and told me when you got out to bring you to her place so she can take care of you."

"You have got to be kidding me. Did she think I would go for that?"

"No, but she made me promise to ask."

Ivy laughed. "You can't say no to my mother, can you?"

"She reminds me of my mother. Every time I go over there she tries to feed me."

"That's a good sign that she likes you."

"Nah, I know she does that to everyone from the mailman to the pest-control guy." He waited a beat. "Antonio called, too."

She blinked. "I'll bet he's having a ball in his new department. Heard through the grapevine he and Denise Williams are an item now."

Tim was uncertain how to respond. He knew how much Antonio hurt Ivy by leaving her, but God forgive him, he couldn't be happier that the man was out of the picture. "He asked me to tell you he called."

"I'll bet."

He was wrong for you, anyway, Tim wanted to say. *Charming, macho, great to look at, but did he know you like I know you? Did he take the time to learn everything, Ivy?* He doubted it. Anybody who knew Ivy wouldn't throw her away like Antonio had.

Ivy remained silent until he guided the truck into the apartment parking lot. Tim opened the door for her and she eased out of the passenger seat. The complex featured an old brick facade, covered by a vigorous scalp of climbing clematis.

They entered the lobby just as a slender young man with dark hair was trying to exit. He screamed and scrabbled past them and down the steps.

Ivy jumped back at his sudden movement, crashing into Tim. She stumbled, but he caught her, holding her against his front for a moment.

Ivy cried out in pain.

The skinny man ran into the yard and folded himself under a picnic table, covering his eyes.

"It's okay, Moe," Ivy said. "I'm sorry we surprised you."

Tim still held her gently, her head tucked under his chin, enjoying the soft feel of her hair on his face. "Is that Moe? I've heard you talk about him. He has a bit of trouble talking to people?"

"Yes. His mother said he has something called Savant Syndrome. People that have it have delays in social reaction and communication, but they can be geniuses in other areas." She rubbed her shoulder. "He's a genius in his own way, even though his communication skills are poor and he's afraid of people. One time I was trying to find a number and he recited the whole *C* section of the phone book. From memory."

"Wow. I can't even remember my own cell number half the time." Tim peered at the figure curled up under the table. "Are you okay, Moe? Do you need some help?" When he received no answer, Tim straightened. "Should we do something?"

"I'll try to talk to him. Moe, this is Tim. He's a friend of mine."

Moe shot them a terrified look and retreated farther under the table. He mumbled something.

"What did he say?"

Tim shrugged. "Numbers, I think. What did you say, Moe?"

The man's mouth worked for a second until he muttered again in a louder voice. "M4e2d7s9c3i6z5t5r472cla0n7noe6r5y9r-9o7w2."

Ivy stared. "That's really, er, interesting, Moe. Do you want to come out from under there? I wanted to ask you something. I thought I saw you at a fire. Was that you, Moe? Were you near a house on Alder Street yesterday?"

He scuttled out the back end of the table, dropping a soda can in the process. With another look in their direction, he snatched up the can and ran.

Ivy sighed. "I check on him once in a while to make sure he's okay and bring him my cans so he can recycle them. He'll come home later, I'm sure, because he's completely addicted to *The Song and the Sorrow*."

Tim blinked. "That soap opera?"

"Yeah. It comes on every weekday at two o'clock. He'll be in his apartment watching it at that time, come rain or shine. I usually just poke my head in and make sure he's all right."

"What does he do on the weekends when it's not on?"

"His mother, Madge, put all the old episodes on tape for him. Fortunately, there are plenty of them. He watches the repeats on Saturdays and Sundays. She checks in pretty frequently. She'll probably call tonight, as a matter of fact. I'll talk to her about seeing him at the fire. Maybe I was mistaken." They stepped into the elevator and pushed the sixth-floor button.

"Oh, wait a minute." Tim poked around in his pocket. "When I came to feed your fish last night, I wrote down a message for you from Madge. I forgot all about it until you mentioned her name." He pulled out a slip of paper. "She said to tell Moe his friend canceled their meeting. Madge asked if you'd seen him around. He's a hippie, a little on the odd side, she said."

The elevator doors opened and let them out into a cream-colored corridor.

"I don't think I've seen anyone like that hanging around with Moe, but I've been working overtime a lot lately."

"I know." Tim gave her a smile. "If I want to see you, I have to go to the station. Anyway, Madge says Moe's friend is an okay guy."

"You and Madge think everyone is okay."

He laughed. "I think you're more than okay."

"Flatterer."

Seeing the flush rise in her cheeks, he knew he'd said too much. He took the keys from her hand and unlocked the door.

Ivy stepped into her cozy apartment and sighed. "It's good to be home."

"Your mom sent over food. I piled it all in the fridge on my way to pick you up at the hospital. She must have been cooking all night." He handed her the keys. "Call me if you need anything at all. I'll come by tomorrow to check on you." *Don't get ahead of yourself, Carnelli. You'll push her further away. You've got a chance, that's all. A chance.* "If that's all right with you, I mean."

"Sure. It's not like I'm going to work or anything."

Tim wanted to fold her into his arms and kiss the sad look off her face. Instead he ventured back into the hallway. She had almost closed the door when a thought popped into his head and he stopped her. "Hey, Ivy. I remembered."

"Remembered what?"

"The name of the guy who canceled the meeting with Moe. It's Cyril."

FOUR

Ivy endured a sleepless night. It was more the mental acrobatics that kept her awake than her injury, although her throbbing shoulder did not help. She could have taken the painkillers prescribed by the doctor, but she figured that mental toughness was a better way to deal with it.

She couldn't get Cyril out of her mind. And Moe. What was he doing at that fire? What was the canceled meeting about? She had the oddest feeling Moe knew something about what happened, something he didn't want to tell. The thoughts finally drove her out of bed.

Before the sun came up, she sat drinking coffee, listening to the fire department traffic on her radio, long before the hallways became busy with the sound of Saturday-morning comings and goings. Someone, her mother most likely, had arranged for a stack of magazines to be left for her with such uplifting content as gardening tips and the top-ten fashion trends of the year. Sandwiched in between the issues was a photocopied article titled, "Dating and the Christian Woman." Her mother's scrawl in the margin said it all.

Ivy, honey, since you're off work for a while, you've got time to have some fun. Kisses, Mama.

Her mother had thrown her matchmaking efforts into overdrive since Ivy's relationship with Antonio went south. She had the sneaking feeling that Mama hadn't approved of her former boyfriend for some reason. Thinking about Antonio set off a memory.

Structure fire. Three alarms before they'd made it on scene.

Her crew was providing manpower, she was new, a probie. The old house was a wreck by the time they got the fire out. The overhaul was nasty, heat trapped in the walls and floors sucking the life out of the on-duty personnel. The call came for them to relieve the attic crew. She found piles of insulation and heavy smoke, blurry figures wielding tools.

Then came Antonio's voice, loud against the din. "Watch out. Holes cut all over this floor, probie."

"Right, Cap," she'd said before she promptly fell up to her waist in a hole. Trapped, unable to raise her arms, she slowly slipped down through to the next floor. Panic, darkness, fear. And then suddenly he was there, catching her by the straps of her airpack and hauling her back up through the hole.

Weeks later, she thanked him again. "I was so scared. Being trapped like that reminded me...well..."

"Don't get all angsty on me, Ivy. I don't deal with worry well. You're much more fun when you're happy."

They'd had fun all right. Until he'd found more fun somewhere else.

She threw the article into the wastebasket. First, she had no desire to date after Antonio took off with another woman. It had taken all her strength to commit to him in the first place and look where that had gotten her. But had she really loved him or merely been drawn to his macho, fun-loving, larger-than-life persona? She wasn't sure, and her uncertainty was another good reason to keep to herself. Her sole concern should be getting her job back.

Second, she wasn't sure she could trust God anymore. She could not stomach giving her faith to such a cruel and indifferent God after what He'd done to Sadie.

She flipped on the TV and settled down to watch something, anything that would take her mind off her troubles. The cheerful lady chatting about how to put some zing into the summer with a snappy new method of faux-finish painting did not engage her. Nor did the old Western or Oregon's newest morning-news duo. Her mind wandered again to the fire.

She could feel the panic at being buried under the piles of

debris, the fear just as tangible as it had been that night. Did Cyril set fire to his own place? Wouldn't be the first time someone had done such a thing to claim the insurance money. The thought sat in her gut like a live grenade. "When I get my hands on that guy, he's going to answer for the damage he's caused."

The ring of the phone startled her.

Tim's voice was cheerful. "Hi, Ivy. I hope I'm not calling too early."

"No, sadly, I've pretty much been up all night."

"Uh-oh. Shoulder hurting?"

"Not much. Mostly I was thinking about Cyril."

"Who?"

"Moe's friend. He's the owner of the house that I nearly died in."

Tim gasped. "Really? I didn't put that together."

"Well, I did, and I'm going to talk to Moe to find out if he knows where his friend might be holed up."

"Okay, but you're going to turn that info over to the police when you find out, right? No taking things into your own hands, John Wayne style?"

"Sure, sure. I'll be good." She looked at the time. It was only nine o'clock. Still five more hours until she could count on finding Moe in his apartment, ready to watch his favorite soap opera. She tuned back into Tim's conversation.

"So do you want to come with me to the game?"

"What game?"

He laughed. "Sometimes I have the strange feeling you don't listen to me. I'm coaching this afternoon. We're two games away from the play-offs. Why don't you come?"

She knew what he was trying to do and it warmed her heart, but the last thing she needed was to be around a bunch of happy parents at a Christian high school, cheering for the kids Tim coached three nights a week. "I think I'm going to take it easy today. I've got to get my shoulder back in shape."

"Oh. Okay."

She felt bad for disappointing him. "Call me after and tell me how it goes."

"Sure. Take care, Ivy."

She tried again to pay attention to the TV with no success. Thoughts of Cyril and Moe kept preying on her mind. She had to know what was going on with the investigation. All at once an idea electrified her. The phone was in her hand almost before she realized it.

There was someone who knew exactly what was going on and he was going to tell her.

In spite of the August heat, Fire Marshal Doug Chee was running fast when Ivy found him later that day. Since her phone calls were routed to his voice mail, she decided on the direct approach. The slender, dark-eyed man would run the track every day whether it was a workday or not. Today he pushed a jogging stroller in front of him with his baby son asleep inside. A little umbrella sheltered the infant, and Ivy noticed that Doug kept to the shaded periphery of the track.

Ivy put herself where he'd see her around the next turn and waited.

He puffed up, stride perfect, a gleam of sweat on his brow. When he saw her, he faltered slightly before he waved and called out. "Hey, Ivy. How's the shoulder?"

"Okay. I need to talk to you, Doug. I tried to call your house, but you weren't in."

"Sorry. It's been crazy busy. I've got two more laps before I've got to go. I'm taking the baby home to Mary in a bit." He passed her and continued on.

Ivy stared at him. She knew Doug was driven and the man had a work ethic second only to her own, but she had a feeling he was only too happy to run away. When he came around the second time, she tried again. "Come on, Doug. This will only take a minute."

He shook his head and sailed on without comment.

By the time he came back the third time she'd decided to play hardball. "You said if there was ever anything I needed, I just had to ask. Remember? I'm asking, Doug."

He slowed to a stop several yards ahead of her and then turned around. "You got me there."

"How is John John?" She peered at the little baby, with his cap of dark hair and the nose so like his father's.

"John John is fine, fine, as we are fond of saying. Thanks to you."

She smiled, remembering the day when they'd arrived to find him barely breathing due to a respiratory infection, mother hysterical, dad trying to remember his infant CPR, hands shaking so badly he could hardly hang on to the baby. She stabilized the child and transported him to the hospital, where he fully recovered. Ivy figured the parents might never do so after a scare like that. "He looks like the strong, silent type."

"As the guy who hands over the 4:00 a.m. bottle, I would have to disagree about the silent part. Anyway, I really do need to get him home, Ivy. So what can I do for you?"

"I want to know what's going on with the investigation. The house on Alder Street?"

"It's pending."

"That's not enough."

He sighed. "Ivy, I like you. You're a ferociously determined person with a heart of gold, but Chief Strong isn't too happy with you right now. She ordered me to keep you out of the whole thing. You understand, don't you?"

Ivy's gut clenched. "I got hurt in that fire. I have a right to know. And a friend of mine is involved. I'm afraid he's headed for trouble."

He rubbed a hand over his chin. "Look, I can tell you it was arson. Does that help?"

"I already knew that. What was the ignition source?"

He laughed. "Nice try. You know I couldn't tell you that even if you weren't in the doghouse with Strong."

"Come on, Doug. Don't I get anything at all? We've worked together for a long time."

"Yes." He sighed. "And you saved my son's life so I'll throw you a bone here, but if this info gets out anywhere, we're both toast. You got me?"

She nodded.

"I'm pretty sure that whoever torched that place was trying to make sure someone died in that fire."

Her mouth fell open. "What? How do you know that?"

"Did you have a hard time opening the bedroom door?"

She recalled it had taken both Jeff and her to pry it open and they'd still had to batter the door across the threshold. "Yeah, as a matter of fact."

"That's because someone jammed something in the frame so tight no one could have gotten it out."

The enormity of it hit her. "So the arsonist was hoping to prevent someone from escaping, probably Cyril, but there was no body recovered. How did he get out?"

"Not sure. It's conceivable they both climbed down the oak tree that's outside his window. It's not an easy climb, but when you're faced with burning to death it might have its appeal. This is all theoretical, of course."

Ivy could picture it. Cyril, in a panic with smoke filling his room, shimmied down the tree and ran. She would make the same risky choice in the face of burning to death, especially with the door wedged shut. "I wonder who wanted Cyril dead."

He pulled the shade more fully over the baby's head. "I don't know, Ivy, but you need to leave that up to the police and on-duty people to find out. You should focus on recovery. And remember, you never heard any of this from me." He jogged away.

Leave it up to the police? Sure, she would, but it wouldn't hurt to look into things since she unfortunately had the time and she had the uneasy feeling Moe was involved. She felt sort of like a big sister to the guy. It pained her to think he might be involved in something he didn't understand.

The lights of the gym were on and she could see movement. She checked her watch. One fifteen. Of course. It was Tim's team prepping for the big game. She had to talk to him about what she'd discovered. He was the best listener she'd ever met and she knew he wouldn't brush her off. Besides, his smile always cheered her up.

Wishing her shoulder would permit her to jog, she headed toward the school. There were a few early birds there but the bleachers were still largely unoccupied. She saw Charlie Gregor, and waved.

"Hey, Charlie. What brings you out for a high-school game?"

Charlie's glasses shone in the overhead lighting. He looked cool in his silk shirt, in spite of the warmth. "Thought I'd check out the local talent. Someday my sister's kids will need to pick a high school."

"You really plan ahead, don't you?"

He laughed. "Nah, it's just an excuse. I will go anywhere to watch a little basketball, pro or otherwise. Want to sit?"

"Sure." She didn't feel like engaging in the usual cheerful banter; her mind was whirling with Doug Chee's revelation. Fortunately, Charlie was uncharacteristically silent.

She didn't recognize Tim at first as she scanned the court. He was barking out commands to the kids working on basketball drills. He joked with them in between, face alight with excitement.

She waited until Tim was alone for a minute.

"Hi, Tim."

His head whipped up from his notes, face breaking into a wide grin. "Hi, Ivy. I didn't think you were going to make it. I'm glad you decided to come watch."

"Oh, well, actually I…" Her words were cut off with the noisy arrival of the opposing team.

He nodded to her. "I've gotta go. I'll talk to you after the game, okay?"

She didn't want to stay in that sweltering gym. She wanted to find Moe and ask him about Cyril, but Tim was already talking with the other coach. With a sigh she returned to the rapidly filling bleachers. A big man wearing a hat and jacket eased his bulk onto the space beside her. Tinted glasses obscured his eyes.

His voice was gravelly. "Going to be a good game, I hear."

"I guess," Ivy said. Her mind returned to the arson fire. She made a note to track down her crew, too, and find out if they knew anything. Saturday night was party night, and a group of firefighters would gather later at a local restaurant for eating and loud music. She'd attended some of the social nights herself, enjoying the camaraderie and the stories, especially if Antonio was there. Now the thought of meeting up with him made her stomach clench. She was glad that he'd transferred departments.

The referee's whistle blew and the court broke into spirited competition. Ivy was sucked into the game in spite of herself. Tim's team played with practiced skill. At the half, they were behind fifteen points, but they rallied to win the game by a scant two baskets.

Tim beamed as he shook the other coach's hand. Bleachers emptied until the court was a mass of happy parents and sweating teenagers. Ivy was surprised when Tim found her in the melee.

"Was that a great game or what?" His face was boyish, flushed with enthusiasm.

Ivy couldn't help but smile. "It certainly was. Congratulations, coach."

He caught up her hand. "Thanks. Hey, we're going out to pizza to celebrate. Come with us."

She squeezed his long fingers for a moment before she let go. "Ah, no, thanks, Tim. I've got something I need to do."

His smile dimmed. "Oh, I forgot. It's party night, huh?"

She nodded. "Do you want to come by after your pizza party? You know the guys all like you." They were polite, certainly, but there was always a feeling that anyone who wasn't in suppression was an outsider. She felt it, maybe even projected it, and she knew that Tim had certainly felt it, too. *He doesn't deserve to play second fiddle to anyone.* The thought startled her.

"No, thanks. I'm going to take Mark to the hospital to see his mom after we eat. She's struggling with breast cancer. I'll catch up with you tomorrow."

She watched him go, his broad shoulders cutting a path through the happy throngs, wondering for a moment if she should have chosen the basketball party.

Ivy stopped to get a drink of water at the fountain before she exited the gym. The parking lot was nearly empty as she made her way along, purse slung over her good shoulder. She let her mind drift as she walked past the lot and onto the grass.

Out of nowhere came the sound of running feet. As she tensed and turned to look behind her, a heavy body plowed into her, knocking her to the ground. Her purse fell underneath her, and she felt hands prodding, scrambling to get a handhold on her bag. She tried to scream, but the man's weight pinned her face to the ground.

Pulse pounding, she tried with all her strength to push him away, but she couldn't budge him. The best she could do was keep curled around her purse as tightly as she could.

No way, creep. You're not going to make a victim of me.

With his fingers wrapped around her hair, her attacker yanked so hard her eyes teared.

It was all she could do to keep fighting.

Just when she thought she would have to give in, she heard a shout.

The weight was lifted off her and she could breathe again. Vaguely she saw a man's figure running away.

Another face peered into hers. "Ivy? Are you okay? It's me."

Through her tears she looked into Antonio's handsome face.

FIVE

Antonio sat with Ivy while she caught her breath. "I came to see the game, but I was too late so I stopped to talk to some friends in the parking lot. Then I saw that guy on top of you. Are you sure you're okay?"

She nodded, wiping the moisture from her face. "Just winded, and my shoulder is throbbing. I thought we were safe from purse snatchings in this small town."

"Guess there's nowhere safe from crime anymore." He hauled her up in his muscular arms and kept her there for a moment. His low whisper tickled her ear. "I was worried when I saw you lying there."

She pulled away. "I thought worry was a feeling you didn't indulge in. Too angsty, or something." Immediately she wished she hadn't said it.

He laughed, his teeth white in the darkness. "Oh, I give worry a few minutes out of my life sometimes. Come on, I'll drive you home. Do you want to call the police first?"

"No. I just want to get out of here. Now."

He led her to his SUV.

She tried to steady her body and emotions as they drove. She could feel a scrape on her knee and various bruises beginning to form.

Antonio eyed her. "Actually, I didn't come just to see the game. I came to check on you."

"Really?" She tried to hide the satisfaction in her voice. "That was nice of you."

"Sure. I'm planning a hiking trip with some of the crew next week. Thought I'd invite you along."

She didn't dare look at him. "How does Denise feel about that?"

He waved a dismissive hand. "We aren't exclusive. She knows that."

She wondered if that's what he told people when they were dating. "Thanks for the offer, but I'm taking it easy on the shoulder for a while."

"Okay."

He chatted away as they drove. Ivy could see why women found him irresistible. She'd thought he was everything she'd wanted in a man, a partner. Was he looking for reconciliation? Was she?

Ivy felt a surge of relief when they pulled into her parking lot and Antonio walked her to the door. Happy as she was to know he missed her, wanted her, she couldn't forget how things had changed.

"If you change your mind about hiking, let me know," he said, giving her a hug.

As quickly as she could, she went inside and closed the door before she said something she might possibly regret.

Ivy felt plenty old the next morning as she eased her arm into the sling after her shower. The sky was a steel gray, indicating a summer storm was on the way. It would be good for the guys, if it brought enough rain to dampen the parched vegetation on the surrounding hillsides.

The phone rang. She figured it was Tim. He made it a point to call every so often on Sundays and invite her to church. She told him in as patient a way as she could that she was not interested. He could go worship God until he ran out of breath. For her part, Ivy was still busy hating Him. Then again, it could be Antonio, she mused.

As she picked up the phone she straightened Sadie's picture, marveling again at how lovely her sister had been, a dark-haired beauty with an easy smile. "Hello?"

A loud breathy voice filled up the phone line. "Hello, Ivy. It's Madge."

Ivy sighed in relief and exchanged pleasant small talk with Moe's mother. "I'm glad you called. I had a question for you. What can you tell me about Cyril?"

"Moe's friend?" Madge paused. "He ran the recycle shack for a while, that's how Moe met him. He worked at the local bookstore, too, I think. But he quit early on. From what I gather he's not above skirting the law a bit, but he's always been sweet to my Moe and that's what matters to me."

"What do you mean, skirting the law?"

"Oh, I've just heard things. I don't want to gossip."

"I understand, but his house burned down, Madge. It would be good if we could locate him."

"My goodness, burned down? He's had a bad string of luck, poor guy. And after getting fired and all."

"Fired? From where? Why?"

"No, now I've said too much. I called to ask you to check on Moe for the next few days. I've got to go visit my sister. She's had surgery you see, for her appendix. I filled Moe's refrigerator and made sure his stock of soap operas is okay. He will call me every night to check in, but I would feel better knowing you'll look out for him."

"Of course I will."

"Good. Do you still have my cell number?"

"Yes. I'll make sure he's okay."

Her relieved sigh was loud. "Thank goodness for you, Ivy. You're a blessing from God. I'll be back in a few days. Bye now."

A blessing from God? Yeah, right.

Ivy spent the next few hours searching the Internet for any information about Cyril. It didn't help that his last name was an unknown. "There are way too many Cyrils in the world," she finally grumped at one thirty as she left her apartment, empty soda can in hand. The hallway was warm and stuffy compared to her air-conditioned unit. She could smell the tang of garlic and ginger from Mrs. Wang's pork dumplings. Her mouth watered at the thought of the succulent pillows and she remembered she hadn't eaten.

She tapped lightly on door 6H. "Moe? It's Ivy. Are you home?"

There was no sound, but that was not unusual. Sometimes it took the man a few minutes to decide to open the door. She knocked again. "Hey, Moe. Your mom asked me to check on you. I wanted to talk before your shows. I know you watch them at two o'clock. I promise I'll make it quick."

The door opened and Moe peered at her, blinking behind his thick glasses. "Ivy? Is that you?"

"Yes, Moe. Are you doing okay?"

He nodded.

"Can I come in?"

"Okay." He moved to the side so she could get by. His apartment was tidy, Spartan almost, with a couch and padded chair the only furniture in the front room, along with a TV. The tiny kitchen opened up onto the space, and she could see he'd already removed the plastic from his microwave-popcorn package and laid the bundle neatly on the counter, ready for popping. His bottle of water sat next to it, carefully wrapped in a paper towel.

"Here's another can for you."

He nodded and added it to a bag near the door. "Thank you."

"How have you been, Moe?"

"Okay." He sat on the sofa, hands folded in his lap.

"Good. Your mom said if you need anything to let me know. Do you remember where my apartment is?"

"Apartment A, floor six, northwest corner of Ash and Finley streets."

"Ah, yeah. Wow. That's it all right." The last time she'd talked to him he'd rattled off a string of bus schedule information. "I wanted to know about your friend Cyril."

Moe stiffened and began to rock slightly back and forth.

Ivy watched his brown eyes as he stared at a spot on the far wall. "Moe, why were you at his house the night of the fire?"

Moe shook his head but did not answer.

Ivy sat down next to him. "I know that he's been missing, Moe. Was he into some trouble? Did he tell you anything about a problem he was having?"

The man began to rock more violently.

"It's kind of important."

"Apartment A, floor six, northwest corner of Ash and Finley streets." He stared into space and repeated the phrase three more times.

Though she felt a surge of frustration, Ivy put a hand gently on his arm, which trembled slightly under her touch. "Okay, Moe. We don't need to talk anymore right now. Why don't you pop your popcorn and watch your show? I'll come back later."

She waited until he had prepared his snack and settled himself into the chair with the remote. He did not turn his head as she said goodbye.

Back in her own apartment there was a message from her mother inviting her to come over. Ivy shuddered. She could not face the idea of sitting at the kitchen table hearing her mother try to encourage her to change careers or find a nice man to settle down with. She had probably already been busy scanning the church directory to look for any eligible men she could find to coerce into taking Ivy on a date.

"I'm a firefighter, Mom," she'd said many times, more frequently since the Antonio debacle. "That's who I am and all I want to be."

She tried to flex her shoulder until the pain stopped her. What was she now? What if she couldn't go back to her beloved calling? The thought froze her insides.

Well, I'm not just going to sit here until I get my job back. She grabbed her keys and headed for the elevator, determined to solve the mystery about Cyril before it got Moe's friend into deeper trouble.

In the car, she turned on her radio pager, listening hungrily to the chatter. The guys were en route to a fire at an office building. Probably nothing major, but listening to the captain radio their ETA made her feel like crying. She could almost feel the quiver in their stomachs as they climbed onto the rig, the rush that came with the chance to knock down a fire. She fought back tears as she turned the key.

* * *

Tim saw Ivy standing on the sidewalk near the burned house, body tense and rigid. It filled him with a desperate desire to lift away her fear, some way, any way. When she didn't hear him speak, he put a hand on her shoulder.

Whirling, she lost her balance and he caught her.

"Sorry, I didn't mean to scare you. What brings you here? What's wrong?"

She leaned her head against his chest for a moment. Then she straightened. "Nothing. I'm fine. I was just… I don't know."

"Remembering?"

"Oh, never mind. How did you find me?"

"I figured it wouldn't take too long before you defied the doctor's orders and drove somewhere. I kind of guessed you'd be back here."

She filled him in on Doug Chee's revelation.

He whistled. "So the door was wedged closed? Kinda shoots down the notion that Cyril torched the place for the insurance money. Somebody went to a lot of trouble to try to kill the guy."

"Or Cyril tried to kill someone and make it look like something else."

"Either way, something didn't go right for somebody." He gave her a sideways look. "I take it you're not going to leave this up to Chee and the police?"

"No. I did talk to the police this morning, though, because some jerk tried to steal my purse last night."

His mouth dropped open. "After the game? What happened? Are you hurt?"

She related the whole story, except the part when Antonio asked her to go hiking with him. At the mention of Antonio's name, Tim's brow furrowed and a dark expression crossed his face.

"Good thing Antonio was there," he said in clipped tones.

"Yeah. Anyway, I figured I'd look into a few things, that's all. While I'm off, I mean."

He smiled. "Well, how about I take you out for some ice cream and we can talk some more?"

"You don't have to entertain me."

"Believe it or not, I like hanging out with you. Usually you're surrounded by people wearing Nomex, and I can't get close unless I happen to be on fire or something." The bitter thought rose before he could stop it. *Even with Antonio gone, you're still out of reach.* He squelched the thought and opened the passenger-side door. "I'll drive."

She opened her mouth to protest, but he propelled her into the seat.

On the way to the ice-cream shop, Ivy asked Tim to stop at Corner Street Bookstore. "I've got to ask Mr. Evans about Cyril. Madge said Cyril worked at the bookstore."

The bookstore owner, Sergei Evans, greeted them with a smile. "Good afternoon."

The shop featured wooden shelves crammed full of books of every description and a long ladder that rolled between them. There was a small section with new bestsellers, but most of the volumes were older, with an occasional antique sprinkled in.

"Hello, Mr. Evans," Tim said.

The man piled his papers in a tidy stack next to the cash register and came around the counter. "Hello. Can I help you find a book?" He looked at Ivy closely as he slipped on wire-rimmed glasses. "I would say you are not the kind who would like to read about needlework or floral arranging."

"You got that right on the money," Tim said as he thumbed through a sports magazine. "The only needles she uses are the kind to administer an IV."

Tim smiled at the look Ivy shot him as they followed Mr. Evans around the small shop.

He pulled a book off a high shelf and handed it to Ivy. "Perhaps a memoir by a blind man who climbed Mt. Everest?"

She took the book and read the back. "That's interesting, but…"

He handed down another. "And maybe a story of Peary's expedition to the North Pole?"

"That sounds great, Mr. Evans, but that's not why we're here," Tim repeated. "Do you happen to know a man named Cyril?"

"Cyril?" He frowned. "A short man, rather fragile-looking?"

Tim nodded, his pulse quickening. The image matched the description Madge had given them.

"He asked me for a job several months back, but I couldn't accommodate him. Why?"

"He's a friend of a friend. We were told he worked here."

"No, I didn't hire him. I had no contact with him after that one encounter."

Tim hid his disappointment. "Okay. Thanks anyway."

Ivy paid for her purchases and they left the cool of the bookstore, practically running into Mitch. He jerked backward.

"Oh, hi, guys."

"Hey, Mitch." Tim noted the weary lines painted on his wide face and felt a tingle of alarm. "Did you have a rough shift? You look beat."

"Shift? No. I'm off for a few days."

Ivy clicked her tongue. "Taking time off isn't going to get you closer to that boat you're after. You need all the overtime you can get."

His brow furrowed. "Who made you my mother?"

Tim blinked at Mitch's tone. "Easy, man. She was just teasing." He gave a half laugh. "Yeah, okay. Sorry."

"How about we all three go get some ice cream?" Tim gestured to Ivy. "We've gotta keep this girl out of trouble."

"No, I can't." Mitch said. "I've gotta run."

Tim tried to read his expression, to see if he was telling the truth, hating the suspicion that clouded his mind. He wished he wasn't burdened by knowing Mitch's secret. "Where are you headed?"

"Me?" He looked momentarily disoriented. "Oh, just out for a jog. Catch you later."

Tim and Ivy walked the rest of the block and ordered ice-cream sundaes, settling at a table by the window to enjoy their treat.

He watched her dive into the sundae, her face as eager as a little girl's. The image tugged at his insides.

Ivy took a spoonful of whipped cream and chocolate sprinkles. "Do you think Mitch is acting funny?"

"Maybe." Tim tried to focus on his black-and-tan sundae, willing her not to ask him anything else. Above all things, he did not want to lie to Ivy.

"Maybe?" She looked closer at him. "Tim? Do you have some idea of what's bothering my cousin?"

"Oh, me? It's not—" He broke off as her attention was riveted to a spot on the sidewalk outside. "What's wrong, Ivy?"

The untouched cream dripped from the spoon suspended in her fingers. "That man. I've seen him before."

Tim looked in the direction of her stare. A big man with blond hair ambled along the sidewalk. He paused for a moment, long enough to sweep his gaze across the window of the ice-cream shop. His eyes rested on the two as they stared back at him. Something in the way he looked at Ivy pricked at Tim. "Who is he?"

Ivy slowly put her spoon down. "I don't know, but he sat next to me at your basketball game last night. I've got a funny feeling."

"What kind of funny feeling?"

"I wonder... Oh, I don't know."

"What?" he prodded.

"I wondered for a second if he was the guy who tried to take my purse."

Tim got up and headed for the door.

"Where are you going?"

"I'm going to talk to him. No harm in that."

"No, Tim. Don't."

Tim ignored her and headed out of the shop. By the time he made it to the sidewalk, the man had already hurried away. He tried not to let his concern show as he returned to the table.

Ivy toyed with her spoon. "Maybe I was mistaken. It was dark and I never saw the purse snatcher's face."

"Maybe." An uneasy sensation took root in Tim's gut. *Maybe not.*

SIX

The clock crept its way to early evening. Ivy tried to keep busy by doing everything from dusting all of her books to reorganizing the spice cupboard.

She was twitchy as a caffeinated cat. She had made no progress on anything, including her healing. Flexing her shoulder brought only a lancing pain that seemed as intense as it had right after the injury.

She was sick of her own company to the point where she actually accepted her mother's invitation to dinner. Granted, it was more an order than an invitation, and since Ivy had no work excuse this time, she made her way on foot over to her mother's house. It was still hot, but a cooling wind whispered through the hemlock trees as she strolled to her mother's block, a strip of tiny, well-kept houses set among massive conifers that seemed to dwarf the whole neighborhood. Many times she'd urged her mother to cut down the branched monster that towered above her roofline with no result.

"At least cut it back, then." She'd seen too many fires jump from canopy to canopy, fueled by hot conditions and Oregon's unpredictable winds.

"Ivy, honey, that can't be done. It's Papa's tree, remember? He used to love to sit and read in the shade or push you girls on the swing. Roddy made a fort up there. I'm not going to touch that tree, and neither is anyone else." Then her mother would smile and politely ignore any further recommendations.

Ivy was so lost in her memories, she stumbled over an uneven spot in the pavement. Recovering her balance, she glanced into the heavily wooded acreage behind the road. Something caught her eye—a flash, a brief glint from the deepest clump of green.

It was almost like… Ivy shook her head to clear it. No way—it couldn't be. Why would someone be out there with a pair of binoculars aimed in her direction? Still, the quick flash bothered her enough that she increased her pace until she was breathless when she arrived at her mother's house.

Juana Beria met her daughter at the door, her round face wreathed in a smile, black hair pulled back in the ever-present knot on the back of her head. Ivy had seen her mother's hair down only twice, once when she was deathly sick with the flu and the other the night of her sister's accident. Even the morning Ivy's dad passed away, her mother met her at the hospital with hair firmly secured.

Squeezed in her mother's well-padded hug, Ivy inhaled the scent of garlic and roasted potatoes from the kitchen behind them. Conversation floated out from the sitting room.

"Who's here, Mama?"

Her mother batted innocent eyelashes. "Just your brother and Mitch."

Ivy heard a familiar deep laugh. "And?"

"And Tim. I haven't seen him in ages. I've got to go check the pie." She padded off, ever the matchmaker.

Ivy couldn't help but smile. When would Mama understand that Tim was just a good friend? Antonio was more her type—charismatic, brash and, most of all, a firefighter. She reminded herself of the sting when she'd shared her feelings with Antonio about their future and he'd run, not walked, to get away from her ideas about commitment. After that kind of humiliation, she didn't want to love anybody.

Still, the sight of Tim's tousled hair and warm grin infused her with happiness.

He hugged her gently, his cheek leaving a warm impression on hers. "How's the shoulder?"

"Rotten. The doctor says I can't even start physical therapy until she gives me the thumbs-up. Who knows when that will be?"

"Oh, that's too bad," Roddy said from his spot by the window. "You're stuck down here with the mere mortals until you rise again as überhero."

"Funny, brother. I just want my shoulder to mend so I can beat you at basketball again."

Mitch grinned as he reached for a chip loaded with salsa. "You did a pretty good job breaking it. Can't expect it to mend overnight."

Ivy was glad to see Mitch's cheerful demeanor. It reminded her that she hadn't fully interrogated Tim about her cousin's strange behavior. "I know, I know, patience and all that. What's the word on the investigation?"

Mitch chewed for a moment. "Why do you ask me? I'm just a flight nurse, not a hose jockey."

She put a hand on her hip and continued to stare.

"You'd better tell her if you know anything," Roddy said. "I've seen that look before."

He sighed. "I haven't heard anything other than the police are involved. Probably just about as much info as you've weaseled out of people." He looked at his watch.

"Got plans?" she couldn't help asking.

"Charlie and I are going fishing tomorrow if the weather holds. I told him I'd get some supplies before the store closes up."

"Since when do you like fishing?"

He smiled. "Since I've matured and appreciate the value of quiet and relaxation."

Ivy sat heavily on a worn recliner. Tim handed her a glass of ice water. They chatted until her mother called Mitch and Roddy into the kitchen.

Ivy got to her feet. "I'll help, Mama."

Juana waved her back. "No, no. You rest your shoulder, baby. Mitch and your brother can help."

Mitch gave her a wink and snatched another chip before he left.

Ivy rose and prowled the room. She often felt restless at her mother's house, afraid the old, familiar surroundings would bring back too many memories. Today she could not fend them off as she wandered along the braided rug, burned on an edge where her father dropped a Christmas candle. Even though she was only five at the time, Ivy remembered the mixture of terror and fascination she felt as the rug caught and a flame erupted before her father stamped it out.

Unwillingly, her eyes were drawn to the photo of Sadie, beautiful Sadie. Unlike Ivy, Sadie's hair was a dark black curtain that fell in a smooth wave. She remembered helping her sister wrap giant pink rollers in her hair only to have her hair fall back into stubborn straightness the next morning. Tim joined Ivy, looking closely at the picture.

"Sadie was a beautiful girl. I wish I could have known her."

Ivy nodded. "You would have liked her. She was fun-loving, a real spark plug." *And a strong Christian, like you are,* she almost added.

"You miss her, don't you?"

Without warning her eyes filled. "The accident happened just before we moved here, fifteen years ago. I still can't believe that much time has passed. Everyone seems to have gotten over it but me. Roddy doesn't even talk about Sadie."

He put his arms around her. "People deal with things in their own way."

She let her cheek rest on his strong shoulder, tears trickling onto his T-shirt.

"She was so young, only eighteen."

"And you were barely twelve." His voice was soft in her ear, soothing like a lullaby. "I can see how a terrible thing like that could change your life."

The anguish she felt suddenly changed to anger. She jerked away from him. "It did change my life, and I know what you're thinking."

He looked puzzled. "What's that?"

"You know. You want to say something about it being God's will and all that."

He blinked. "No, I wouldn't presume to speak for God, Ivy. I just know He loves you and feels your heartbreak."

"Well, I don't want Him to love me. I won't love Him back, do you hear? You can sing His praise until the cows come home, Tim, but I won't love a God who tortures people like that." She rubbed a hand over her wet eyes, shocked at her emotional outpouring.

Tim sighed. "I know you're angry, Ivy, and hurt. I would give anything to help take some of your pain away, I really would."

The look he gave her was so tender, so honest, that she felt a stab of regret for her outburst. She wanted suddenly to snuggle in his arms and return to the comfort she found there.

Her mother poked her head into the room. "Come to dinner."

Grateful for the interruption, Ivy led them into the kitchen. They squeezed in next to Mitch and Roddy at the table.

Ivy was happy to focus on the food and conversation after her unsettling connection with Tim. She could still feel his arms around her and part of her felt quivery inside. She tried to savor her mother's golden-brown potatoes and succulent roast.

Tim passed around a bowl of peas. "How's the writing coming, Mrs. Beria?"

"Just fine, thank you, Tim. I'm so pleased when kids e-mail to tell me they enjoy the stories or send in questions and things."

Ivy swallowed hard. Her mother began writing a serial story called Penny Pocket for the local paper several years ago, modeling the little girl protagonist after Sadie. She'd explained it was therapeutic, God's way of helping her help other children. Ivy had read only one installment, recognizing instantly her sister's bubbly personality shining through the lines. Ivy faithfully clipped every one out of the paper, putting them unread into a box under her bed.

Roddy's gaze was drawn to the window. "Are you expecting someone else, Mama?"

"No, honey. Why?"

"I thought I saw that car pass by a couple of times. I figured you'd invited someone and they're looking for your house."

Ivy's instincts prickled. She walked to the window and

peered out. A dark sedan was just disappearing around the corner. It was too far away to make out any details. Could it be the man who'd mysteriously appeared at the basketball game and the ice-cream parlor?

Tim exchanged a glance with her, and she knew he was wondering the same thing.

She was startled to find Mitch right behind her, staring out the window, his face painted with fear.

He spoke to Roddy over his shoulder while continuing to look out the window. "Who was driving? Did you see?"

Roddy helped himself to more potatoes. "No. Didn't get a look. Why?"

Mitch shook his head. "No reason. No reason."

Ivy saw the bead of sweat that rolled down Mitch's temple as he went back to his seat. She tried to catch his eye but he sat, looking at his plate and gulping down ice water. *He's terrified about something, and I'm going to find out what it is.*

Ivy didn't get the chance to press her cousin. After dinner she found herself elbow to elbow with Tim, handing him dishes at the sink. By the time they'd finished, Mitch had already gone.

"He didn't say goodbye. Where did he go?"

Her mother shook her head. "He said he had to do some paperwork before he got the fishing supplies, and away he went."

"That's funny. Mitch hates to do paperwork on his days off so he usually stays late to get it done during his time at work." Ivy cast a glance at Tim, who was busily chatting with Roddy. She kissed her mom and got ready to leave. "Tim, do you want to walk with me?"

"I can go partway," he said, after a moment's hesitation.

Plenty of time to get the truth out of him.

Tim started talking as soon as their feet hit the sidewalk. Ivy let him go on for a while before she corralled the conversation. "Let's have it, Tim. What's the matter with my cousin?"

Tim's eyes widened. "Why would you think I'd know that?"

"Because you and Mitch used to be best friends."

He looked toward the trees, outlined by the setting sun. "We aren't so close anymore."

"Why not?"

"He developed other interests."

"What interests?"

Tim sighed. "Look, Ivy. I can't tell you for two reasons. It's not my place to talk about your cousin. If you want to know what's going on in his life, you'll have to ask him. Otherwise, it's just gossip on my part."

"What's the second reason you can't tell me?"

"I've got a quick coach's meeting. Do you want to come?"

She declined.

"I'm not sure it's a good idea for you to walk alone," he said.

She bristled. "I'm a tough cookie, Tim. I don't need a bodyguard."

"At least call my cell when you get home so I know you got there safely." He gave her a squeeze and trotted off across the empty field toward the school gym.

Ivy swallowed her frustration. As she covered the remaining half mile home, she wondered again about the man who she'd seen lurking around town. Was he the would-be purse snatcher? Or maybe he was part of her cousin's new "interests," whatever those were.

She lay on the couch for a while, tired and grumpy, her stomach complaining about the amount of her mother's delicious dinner she'd put into it. Finally hauling herself to her feet, she went to Moe's apartment and gently tapped on the door.

There was no answer.

On her way back to her own apartment, fumbling for her keys, she did not hear the sound of soft-soled shoes on the carpeted corridor. The hand that grabbed her from behind was strong and ice cold.

SEVEN

Ivy spun around and screamed.

The man cried out and fell back a step, flattening himself against the corridor wall. He was short, balding on the top, dark eyes settled close together above a large nose. His mouth twitched and moved as if he were saying a silent confession.

"What do you want?" Ivy finally managed. "Who are you?"

He shook his head, darting a glance down the hallway. "Tell him to hide what I gave him. Don't let anyone take it."

"Who?"

The man's eyes widened in frustration. "Moe."

A realization struck her. "Are you Cyril?"

He didn't answer, only shivered slightly and took a few steps away from her.

"Wait a minute. Did you set fire to your house?"

"No."

"Is someone trying to kill you?"

He looked behind him and tensed. "I've got to go. Tell him."

"Hold on," she called as he took off. She jogged after him, plunging down the stairs in pursuit. His shoes pounded down the steps, heedless of the noise.

She gripped the rail with one hand and held her injured arm against her side as she careened down after him.

He burst onto the grounds a second before her. It was almost completely dark, the bare light from a half moon painting his features in stark terror. "I have to get out of here. Just tell him,"

Cyril whispered fiercely before he turned and whirled away into the woods behind the apartment building.

Ivy watched for a moment to detect which way he'd gone. Then her situation settled around her like a heavy cloak. She was alone, in the dark, having just met a man who was running for his life. Then again, maybe she wasn't alone. Her skin prickled in terror. Whomever Cyril was fleeing from might be watching, waiting for a moment to snag her, too.

She couldn't go back up the stairwell into that dark space. The front door to the lobby would be deserted as well. She fumbled for her cell phone. Tim, she had to call Tim. A moment later that hope was dashed. He was at the gym, and she knew he always turned off his phone there.

The car. She'd make it to the car and drive to the school. Flesh tingling with fear, she tried to look in all directions as she made her way through the parking lot to her covered space. The figure of a man detached itself from the shadows. Her mouth rounded in a terrified scream even as she prepared to run.

Tim saw her dart into the parking lot as he pulled up. He'd been right to come and check on her. Her fear was palpable, even from a distance. "Ivy?"

She threw herself in his arms, nearly knocking him over.

"What is it? What's wrong? Are you all right?" He tried to pull her to arm's length, but she clung to him tight until she was able to take a shuddery breath.

"It was Cyril. He's on the run."

Tim waited until she'd gotten out some of the strange story. He could feel her shivering against his chest. "Cyril came here?"

She nodded. "He was terrified."

He was silent for a moment, eyes shifting in thought. "Okay. I'm going to walk you up to your apartment and I think you'd better pack some things and go stay with your mother tonight, right after we call the police."

He let her in and checked the small space. Everything was untouched, no sign of a stranger's intrusion.

She gasped. "Tim. I just thought of something. What about Moe? Why didn't Cyril just talk to him? Do you think he's okay?"

"As a matter of fact, I know he's okay. I just saw him."

"Where?"

"On the way over here I saw Moe and his mother at the ice-cream shop. I said hello and introduced myself. Madge said to tell you her sister had so many church people helping her out there was no need to stay so she's back in town. Moe is going to sleep at her house for a few days."

Ivy sagged in relief, collapsing onto the sofa. "Cyril gave him something and my guess is somebody wants it back. At least Moe's safe for the night. We'd better call him tomorrow, too."

Tim pushed his own growing concern aside and took her hand. "We'll get this all straightened out, Ivy."

She swallowed. "I've changed my mind. I'm sure I'll be fine here tonight. I don't need to go to my mother's."

He folded his arms, not surprised by her sudden refusal. "Yes, you do."

"I promise I'll lock the door."

"Uh-uh. You're going to your mom's."

She raised an eyebrow. "Really? And what if I don't?"

"I'll call your mother and tell her the situation."

"And what if I still don't agree?"

He considered for a moment. "Then I'll throw you over my shoulder in a perfect fireman's carry and lug you down to the car myself. You can kick and scream but one way or another, you're going."

"You would do that?"

"To keep you safe? Oh, yeah. I would do that."

She watched him, wide-eyed. "Okay. I'll go pack a few things."

"Very good choice."

Detective Spencer Greenly laced his fingers across his wide belly as he listened to Tim and Ivy tell the story. A gum-wrapper chain looped through the top handle of his file cabinet.

Tim wished he could read the expression on his face, but it was impossible. Occasionally he tamped down his salt-and-pepper mustache and made a note on his yellow pad.

Ivy told Greenly about Moe, his relationship with Cyril and proximity to the fire.

Tim added a few details to complete the picture, including the dangers Ivy had encountered.

With a sigh, the detective unwrapped a piece of gum and shoved it in his mouth. He noted their looks. "Trying to quit smoking. So you think Cyril is being followed?"

Tim frowned. "Well, someone is after him, and I'm afraid they are going to go after Moe since apparently Cyril gave him something."

Greenly's look gave nothing away. "We'll talk to Moe, but you say he's pretty…noncommunicative?"

Ivy joined in. "Strangers scare him. It took three years before he'd talk to me, and I'm his neighbor."

The officer nodded. "I'm sure his mother will let us into the apartment to take a look around. Did Cyril say what he'd given to Moe?"

Ivy shook her head. "No. He was in a real hurry to go. I don't think he intended to talk to me at all, but Moe wasn't home so he got desperate."

Tim shifted on the hard chair, stomach clenching with the thought. "I'm concerned that Ivy is in some kind of danger."

"Hard to say. In view of the fact that someone tried to burn down Cyril's house with him inside, I'd say Cyril is the one in real danger at the moment. Just to be sure, we'll assign someone to drive by her complex and keep an eye on things when they can."

Tim leaned forward. "Will that be enough?"

The barest of smiles curled Greenly's mustache. "It will have to be. This isn't exactly a bustling department. We've only got three officers and a staff of volunteers. Our most faithful volunteer traffic officer just turned seventy-two.

"Before you go, take a look at this for me." Greenly opened

a file and slid a picture across the table to them. "Recognize this guy? Is he the one who was following you?"

"No, but I saw him at the basketball game. Who is he?"

"He goes by a lot of names. Sam Shoemaker is his current nom de plume. He's connected to some bad people, people who don't like to be cheated out of what's theirs."

Tim started as though he'd been given an electric shock. A suspicion flared in his brain like a flame flicking to life. "Like the mob?"

"Exactly like the mob. We've been aware that he's been in town for a few weeks. Got an officer keeping tabs on him as much as possible. So far he's not guilty of anything, but there's got to be a reason he's come to our sleepy hamlet. Next time you see him, call me immediately." He handed Ivy and Tim his card. "He's not the kind of guy you want to have a chat with, you know?"

He had no doubt the detective was right.

Ivy shook her head as they left. "What's going on here, Tim? This is turning into a real mess."

He pulled her closer as they walked to the truck, wishing he could keep her there, tucked into the protection of his arms. "I hope for Cyril's sake the cops figure it out soon."

When they arrived at Ivy's mother's house, Tim lingered in the doorway, enjoying the nearness of her and wishing that he could prolong the feeling.

"Thanks for the ride," she said, taking a step away from him. "This alpha-male thing was a fluke. Don't get used to bossing me around."

He smiled. "I would never boss you around unless it was for your own good."

"So you think you know what's good for me?"

Looking into her green eyes, he felt his heart expand to fill his chest. He cupped her face with his hands and felt her cheeks warm, infusing his fingers with a gentle heat. "No, but I'd sure like a shot at making you happy."

"You're my best friend. You do make me happy."

I could be so much more than that, if you'd let me. He leaned over and stroked the smooth skin of her cheek. "Good night, Ivy. You'll be in my prayers."

EIGHT

Tim met Ivy back at her apartment the next afternoon, note-pad in hand.

"I want to go on record as saying this is a bad idea."

"I'll be fine, really." It galled her that she'd been scared out of her own apartment. In the light of day, the whole thing seemed ludicrous. Plus his touch the night before had made her feel wobbly inside and she was determined to take control of her life and her feelings. She eyed his skeptical expression. "The police are going to drive by to check on things, remember?"

He frowned. "Yes, the mostly volunteer, severely understaffed department that's already handling an arson, looking for Cyril and keeping track of a mobster. Why doesn't that comfort me?"

She handed him a cup of coffee. "Don't worry so much. You'll get wrinkles."

He uncapped a pen and began to jot. "I thought we could make a list of things we know about Cyril and maybe do some snooping around on our own, the safe, cyber kind of snooping, I mean."

Her heart lifted. "Really? You can do that?"

He huffed. "Don't underestimate me, Beria. There are some advantages to being a techno-geek. You hero types may get all the kudos, but you'd be surprised what a person can accomplish with some computer skills."

She sat next to him. "I'll be more than surprised if you can crack this case. Greenly told us Cyril's last name is Donovan. Madge said he's known Moe for five years or so."

Together they brainstormed a scant list of details about the mysterious man.

"Oh, and he was fired from a job, I think Madge said, but she wouldn't tell me where."

"Okay, that's a start. I'll try to find out what I can." Tim glanced at his watch. "I've got a game this afternoon, so we'll have to pick this up tonight."

"Why don't I come?" She knew a couple of the guys from work would be there and she desperately wanted to close the gap that seemed to be growing between herself and her career. She felt a stab of guilt to see Tim's face light up.

"You want to cheer us on? Great. I didn't think you were interested."

You should be, Ivy. You should want to go for Tim's sake, not for selfish reasons. "Sure. I'll come and root, root, root for the home team, as they say."

He nodded, still grinning, and gathered up his papers.

They took the elevator downstairs and drove to the high school.

Ivy took her place in the stands. Surreptitiously she scanned the bleachers for the stranger. He would probably not risk making himself too obvious. He'd already ascertained that Cyril didn't hang around the basketball court. Then again, she thought with a shiver, he may have been watching when Cyril showed up at the apartment, in which case she'd be a target now. Maybe he'd go after more than her purse this time. She shivered.

The home and visiting teams piled onto the court, sneakers squeaking against the waxed floor. Ivy waved to Jeff and his wife, who came to sit with her.

Jeff shook his head. "Man, Ivy, things aren't the same without you."

She couldn't hide her smile. "I'm glad. I was afraid you didn't even notice I was gone."

"Oh, we noticed. I've been going crazy trying to cover your workload, too, until they…" He broke off, a guilty look in his eyes.

"Until what?"

Jeff's wife patted her knee. "Nothing, Ivy. Jeff is just babbling away. Too much coffee and he turns into a chatterbox."

Ivy raised an eyebrow. "I don't think it's the coffee. What is it, Jeff? What don't you want me to know?"

"Oh, it's not important. Don't sweat it, Ivy." He made a great show of watching the kids drill. "Wow, look at that rebound. Tim's really got them whipped into shape."

"Jeff, if you don't tell me, I'm going to have to post the story to *Firefighters Online*. You know the one I mean." She saw it clearly in her mind.

The deck gun on Engine Five was leaking. Jeff turned it on to show the maintenance guy and it came loose, falling directly into the open cab. The front end flooded with gallons of water. When the captain opened the door to survey the damage, a waterfall of gear including the battalion chief's helmet came pouring out all over the place. Every time they'd turned on the siren for months afterward, the thing sounded like a whale with intestinal problems.

She fought to keep the smile off her lips at the memory.

He blanched. "Now, that's low, Ivy. You wouldn't dare. They only recently stopped calling me Noah."

She folded her arms.

Jeff cleared his throat. "It's no big thing, anyway. Strong just brought in someone to backfill, while you're healing."

She had expected that much. "Who?"

"Uh, well, you know…"

"Who?"

He exhaled loudly. "Williams."

Her stomach clenched like a fist. Denise Williams was a firefighter with a neighboring county who had tried to get on with Ivy's department for years. She was also the woman who had stolen Antonio from her. She was sharp, competent and aggressive, a woman who knew an opportunity when she saw one. Though Ivy no longer loved Antonio, the hurt and humiliation remained. Now Denise was trying to take her job as well?

When she didn't reply, Jeff gave her good shoulder a playful punch. "Don't worry, Ivy. It's not like Strong is going to replace you or anything."

Ivy clenched her jaw. Why shouldn't Strong replace her? If Ivy couldn't get her shoulder back to one hundred percent, she would have no other choice. Not to mention the fact that the chief was no doubt still angry about Ivy's insubordination. Why wouldn't she be giving Denise Williams a good shot at Ivy's job?

The conversation was replaced by cheers and shouts as the game started. Ivy felt detached from it all. Her job, her everything, was floating further out of her reach like a toy boat being towed out by an ocean riptide. Her shoulder began to throb with a painful rhythm. In a daze she watched Tim's team put up a valiant effort only to lose by five baskets.

"Come on over to our house," Jeff said after the final whistle. "The guys are showing up for pizza and a Wii bowling tournament later."

She forced a smile. "Oh, no, thanks. I'm going to stick around and wait for Tim. He's giving me a ride home."

"Okay." Jeff gave her a worried look as he and his wife climbed down from the risers. "If you change your mind, you know where to find us."

She waited as the gym began to empty. More than anything, she wanted to talk to Tim to hear his comforting reassurance that things were going to be okay. She wondered when she started to care so much about his input.

He trotted out of the locker room minutes later, checking his watch. She congratulated him on a good effort.

"Thanks. The kids played well and I'm proud of them." He looked at the door. "Jeff said the guys were going over to his place. I figured you'd be going with them."

"I didn't feel like it. Want to walk with me?"

"Uh, well, I can't actually. I promised the kids I'd stop by the pizza party to celebrate a good season."

"Okay. I can wait while you chow down a slice of pepperoni."

He shifted from one foot to the other. "Actually, I've sort of got this other thing I need to do, but I don't think you should walk home alone."

She blinked. "Oh, don't worry about me. If you've got other plans, no biggie. I was going to go by my mother's house anyway."

"You sure?"

"Sure, no problem. Are you, er, meeting someone?"

"Yeah. Call me when you're finished at your mom's and I'll drive you home."

"Okay." She was dying to ask him who he was meeting, but he'd already headed for the door.

She mused as she left the gym. Tim had an appointment. Was he on his way to a date? She knew plenty of women who would be interested in him. He was sweet, honest and had principles—perfect boyfriend material for someone in the market for that kind of thing. She'd thought so before she met Antonio.

No, it was probably some small group Bible meeting, but that was usually on Thursday nights, she knew. Why had he looked so anxious about it? And why did a stab of jealousy seem to shrink her insides? Jealousy came with love, didn't it?

The cool of the early evening felt delicious after the stuffy gym. A slight humidity tinged the air. She stood for a moment, feeling lost as she watched the people empty out and return to their respective lives. If she wasn't a firefighter, then who was she? What was she supposed to be doing with her life?

Though her plans to see her mother had been in the formative stages only, she decided to make good on what she'd told Tim. Going back to her empty apartment and stewing about Denise Williams would not accomplish anything. Picturing Tim on a date would not be helpful, either. The streets were quiet except for the leaves chattering in the branches. She looked over her shoulder for any sign of an attacker.

Without warning, her anxiety came out in words. She turned her face to the clouded sky. "So what are You doing up there, God? Is this just another way to punish me? When You took my sister, You gave me a calling, as least I thought You did." Her voice rose against the wind. "Aren't I supposed to be out saving lives and property? Isn't that it, Lord? Now You're going to rip that away, too? The only thing I have?" *And maybe Tim, too?* she added silently. She wanted to hit, strike out at something, someone. The only sound came from the swirl of leaves on the fingers of a playful wind.

Head bowed, fatigue soaking into every muscle, she closed the distance to her mother's house.

Her depression was complete when she read the note propped on the kitchen table.

Sorry, Ivy honey, if you came. I wasn't sure and the pastor asked me to take a meal to Mrs. Ronald, who has broken her leg in a fall. I left a sandwich in the fridge for you in case you made it here. Take care and I'll phone you tomorrow. Mama

Mrs. Ronald was no doubt being deluged with pots of soup, containers of casserole and plates of cookies from Mama's church folk. She'd better heal before she ate herself to death. Ivy pulled out the sandwich. Though she wasn't hungry, she took a few bites anyway, trying to take comfort from the familiar old table, knicked from the time she and Sadie used it for a Daniel Boone fort and the cupboard that they'd loved to empty and transform into a cave.

She was surprised when her brother let himself in the front door.

"Hi, Roddy. What brings you here?"

"Oh, hey, sis. Mama asked me to drop off a bag of lemons from my tree. Something about lemon bars. I told her fine as long as I get a couple dozen."

He sank down next to her at the table.

She held up her dinner. "Want half a sandwich?"

"Sure, thanks. I can only stay a minute but there's always time for food."

They enjoyed a comfortable silence as they ate.

As she chewed, her thoughts returned to her sister. How would she have turned out? Would she be a teacher as she'd been studying to do? Or a circus clown, the silly dream she'd clung to since she was a preschooler? Sadie's face swam into her vision, Sadie with her nose covered in red lipstick, trying to juggle oranges in the backyard. Sadie, who died with no one to comfort her, not so much as a squeeze from her sister's hand.

Ivy put down the remaining crust of bread. "How come it didn't change you?"

Roddy looked startled. "What?"

"Sadie's death. You don't talk about it."

He shifted on the chair. "I'm not a 'talk about your feelings' kinda guy, Ivy. You know that."

"I know, I know. But didn't it mess you up at all?"

He considered, his eyes searching her face. "Sure. It was terrible. I don't dwell on it."

"You don't dwell on it?" She was suddenly angry. "She was our sister. How can you just put her out of your mind like a bad meal or a disappointing football game?"

Roddy sighed, wiping his hands on a paper napkin. "I didn't say I put her out of my mind. I loved Sadie. I enjoy reliving the moments we had together, the fun we had as a family. I choose to remember how she lived, not how she died. If you only stay rooted in that moment she was killed, you kind of disrespect her life, you know?" He got up from the table and kissed the top of her head. "Ivy, I know it was hard for you, being there when it happened and all, but Sadie loved life and she wouldn't have wanted you to spend the rest of yours grieving."

She watched him go, afraid to speak because of a sudden thickening in her throat.

At the door, Roddy paused. "I love you, Ivy. We all do. Remember that."

The door closed softly behind him.

Ivy wanted to cry, to let out all the pain that seemed to fester inside her. No, more than that, she wanted to work. To polish the rig until it shone. To answer a call and see the relief on the victim's face when they pulled up. To make the big save and bring someone back.

The darkness closed in around her. She flipped on the lights to dispel the gloom.

She wandered around the house until she came to the window facing the garden. A movement caught her eye. Nerves tingling, she ducked behind the curtain. What had she seen?

A man's silhouette? No, surely not.

Her fingers were clumsy with fear as she scrambled to check the lock on the sliding door and windows. Returning to the garden window, she moved the curtain a tiny fraction and peered out.

She saw only the dark shapes of her mother's tomato plants bobbing in the slight wind.

Squeezing her eyes shut, she tried to recall exactly what she'd seen.

It was just a shadow, a dark shape that had showed briefly against the moonlight. There was no reason to think it was anything but a cat or maybe the neighbor's dog. Then why did her heart still jackhammer in her chest? She remembered the strange glint she'd seen earlier that made her think someone was watching her with binoculars. Paranoia seemed to be creeping in from all sides.

"You're being an idiot, Ivy. You're still freaked about that guy who tried to steal your purse. There isn't a stalker hiding behind every shadow." With a deep breath she peeked out into the yard again. Nothing. Flipping on the outdoor lights revealed nothing either. With a sigh of relief she headed to the phone and dialed her mother's cell.

"No, nothing's wrong, Mama. I thought I saw something in your yard, but there's nothing there now. I just wanted to tell you, you know, be careful, just in case." She felt foolish. She was turning into an hysterical female.

Her mother didn't seem to be too flustered. "Lupe's with me anyway. She's going to spend a few nights with me because her house is being tented for termites."

Ivy felt better as she hung up with her mother. Even though there had been nothing in the yard, she was glad to know her mother would have company for the next few days. A knock at the door ripped through her calm.

Who would be visiting this late?

She crept softly to the door, heart pounding, cell phone ready to dial for help. At first she could not identify the figure with head bowed on the doorstep. Then with a surge of profound relief, she opened the door to Tim.

"Hey, Ivy. I saw the lights on. Thought I'd check in."

"Are you done with your appointment already?"

"Yeah, uh, went quicker than I thought."

His voice sounded odd, tight with some repressed emotion.

"Is…everything all right?"

"Sure, sure. Are you determined to go to your apartment?"

"You bet. Mama's out on a mission of mercy. Can you give me a lift? Come in while I turn off the lights." She decided not to tell him about her silly fears. It was paranoia, pure and simple.

"I'll wait here. I don't want to track dirt on your mother's floor."

His lack of resistance to taking her home took her by surprise. Though she thought it was strange, she did not press him.

On the way to her apartment, she tried to pinpoint what was wrong, but it eluded her.

"Did Jeff talk to you about Denise?"

"Yeah. He told you, too, huh?"

Tim nodded. "He wasn't sure how you were going to take it."

"Take it? How are you supposed to take having someone try to steal your job? Your life?" *Your boyfriend?*

They reached the parking lot and continued on foot to her building. The sky was an inky black.

"I'm sure Denise knows you're coming back," Tim said.

"She'd better. Without my job, I'm… I don't know what I am."

Tim sighed deeply. "You're so many things besides a fire-fighter, Ivy."

Normally, his remark would have irritated her, but the sadness in his voice caught her by surprise. "You're wrong, Tim. I'm a firefighter, that's all I am and that's all I want to be."

"You've been hurt, losing Sadie, losing Antonio, but that

doesn't reduce you to a job. You're still supposed to live, love and laugh, all that good stuff. There are jobs for you that you haven't even imagined yet."

She wasn't sure how to respond as they walked upstairs and he unlocked her door. He did a careful check of the place.

His back to her, he said, "Looks okay. Sleep well, Ivy. Things will feel better in the morning."

"Wait, Tim." She put a hand on his back to stop him. The band of shoulder muscles tensed like steel under her fingers.

"I've really got to go."

"Not until you turn around."

With his broad shoulders slumped he slowly turned until the kitchen light shone on his face.

She gasped, finally understanding why he had been keeping to the shadows.

NINE

Tim felt a sudden feeling of defeat overtake him. He sighed.

Ivy gasped. "What happened to you?"

He waved her hand away. "It's nothing. I'm fine."

"From where I'm standing it doesn't look fine."

He allowed her to take his arm and guide him onto the sofa, turning his cheek to the lamplight. "It looks like you took a punch to the eye."

He shrugged, leaning his head back on the cushions. "Something like that."

She retrieved an ice pack and pressed it to his face. "Who hit you?"

He gave it one last try. "Why do you assume someone hit me? I could have run into something. We both know I'm not exactly grace in motion."

"But you didn't, and since you can't lie to save your life, you might as well come clean."

He propped his elbows on his knees with a sigh. "I can't tell you."

Her eyes narrowed. "Why not?"

"Because I just can't, that's all." He got up and took the ice pack back to the sink. "I think I'd better go."

"Wait, Tim." She turned him to face her. "If I showed up with a black eye and refused to tell you what happened, you'd freak out."

He felt a torturous mixture of frustration and tenderness. For a split second, he allowed himself to consider how he'd feel if someone struck her. He reached out a finger and traced her cheek.

"If someone hit you, I'm afraid I would forget my self-restraint and knock his block off."

She captured his fingers in hers. "So tell me."

His heart sped up, but he kept his voice level. *Lord, help me handle this right,* he prayed. "I am trying to help someone who doesn't want my help and that someone's situation is their business and theirs alone."

"Your principles are maddening."

He grinned. "And painful sometimes."

She looked closely at the wound and he knew she was checking his pupils for signs of concussion. He didn't have one, he was sure, but if that kept her there, close to his face, her mouth inches from his, he wouldn't tell her otherwise.

"Well, at least tell me you're not going to help this person out anymore, right?"

"No can do."

She blew out a breath. "Be reasonable. If someone is going to clobber you, they don't deserve your help."

"I'd like to agree with you but the Bible says differently."

Ivy turned away. "Come on, Tim. You know the Bible is just a book to me now. A bunch of pages and a cover, that's all."

If I could only show you how powerful those words are, Ivy, you could let go of your pain. He put a hand on her back and leaned his face on her shoulder. "If someone strikes you on the right cheek, turn to him the other also." He whispered gently in her ear. "I will always be there to give you my other cheek, Ivy, if that's what you need to learn to love Him again." He gathered her close and breathed in the scent of her.

She pushed him away. "Leave me alone about God, Tim. He's not benevolent, as least not to me."

The frustration swirled through him again. Longing and loving were not enough. As much as he wanted to, he could not help her and it killed him. Only God could turn her heart. He would try, though. The words pained him even as he prayed them. *Lord, help me to be what she needs me to be, even if that's only a friend.*

"Good night, Ivy." Tim closed the door softly behind him.

* * *

Nick sighed. It would have been much easier if he'd snatched Cyril's friend at the fire. The guy ran like a rabbit, too fast for Nick to track. He seemed an unlikely friend for Cyril, but Nick had followed Cyril enough to know that the guy was a chameleon who could creep from place to place and blend in with the surroundings. Cyril was smart, too smart.

It just didn't pay to be too smart.

Nick did not consider himself a smart man, but he had a character trait that made up for that. Determination. He was determined not to return to digging postholes and the odd grave for a living. The work had given him steel muscles and an inexhaustible tolerance for bitter cold and sizzling heat, but it was not a job that would carry him to old age. Nick was smart enough to know that.

This life in Oregon suited him just fine. The variety kept it interesting and the mobile trailer parked on the back of the property was plenty big for a hot plate and TV. He didn't even mind the ever-present threat of rain. He enjoyed the adventure, such as the purse snatching and spying on the girl earlier at her mother's house. Too bad she'd left before he'd picked her lock.

He sat under the canopy of a sprawling pine and watched the entrance to the apartment. A tall man with a shiner came out before eight and left without noticing Nick.

Mind wandering, he wondered again what the constant ebb and flow of humanity looked like from a distance. Ants, he decided. It would look like a colony of busy ants, trailing back and forth on endless forays. The thought amused him as he sat. It was time to step up the pace, he thought. Get busy, like those ants.

The nighttime brought a coolness that he would have found refreshing if temperature impacted him in the slightest way. He settled himself more comfortably against the broad tree trunk and turned his thoughts to cameras while he waited.

Ivy heard the scream that night. It came from the hallway, a long, vibrato wail that made her hair stand on end. She threw open the door and hurtled out. Moe's apartment door was open and he stood in a corner trembling, flapping his hands up and down as if he were fanning some kindling to life.

His mother leaned against the doorway with her hands over her mouth.

Ivy gasped at the ruins that lay everywhere. The drawers were emptied, cushions torn off the sofa and Moe's precious video collection tossed over the carpet.

Madge looked up when she saw Ivy. "We came over to pick up a few things, but Moe was hungry so I took him out for a slice of pie first. We weren't gone for more than two hours. Who would do something like this?"

Ivy checked her watch. Almost ten thirty. How had someone gotten in and out, unnoticed? She hadn't heard anything unusual, but then again she'd been in the shower so she'd made her own noise. "I'm going to call the police. Why don't you come to my place so you don't disturb any evidence?"

Madge eyed her son, who was rocking from foot to foot, his face a mask of anguish. "Let me see if I can calm him down a little first. He won't want to move for a while."

Ivy nodded and placed one call to the police and one to Tim. Then she returned to wait with Madge and Moe.

They showed up within minutes of each other.

Greenly made a few attempts to talk to Moe. He gave up quickly and shoved a piece of cinnamon gum into his mouth before he started to photograph the room. Madge took Moe's hand and managed to pull him to the couch.

Tim jogged up the stairs, wearing jeans and a T-shirt. The bruise was now vivid against his fair skin. His worried eyes sought hers. "Is everyone okay?"

Ivy nodded and joined him in the hallway. "Somebody broke into Moe's place."

He glanced around her into the room. "Looking for something, I see."

Ivy remembered Cyril's frightened face from their meeting in that same hallway.

"Do you think Moe will tell Greenly if he's got something of Cyril's?"

They looked at the trembling young man.

Ivy sighed. "Maybe his mother can figure out what's going on."

Madge couldn't. She led her son into the hall. He stood rigid as plaster, whispering to himself. "The officer agreed to let us back in when he's done so I can get some of Moe's things. He's going to come stay with me until this mess is sorted out."

Ivy kept her voice low. "Do you have any idea what Cyril might have given to Moe?"

"He gave him lots of things. A picture frame, a checker game, little odds and ends like that. All junk. Nothing that anyone would go to this trouble to find." She pursed her lips. "To do this, to someone like my Moe who never causes anyone trouble." Tears crowded her eyes.

Ivy put an arm around the woman's padded shoulders. "I think it has more to do with Cyril than Moe."

Tim nodded. "Just the same I think it's a good idea to take him to your house."

Greenly gave the all clear, and Madge led Moe back into the apartment to pack his things.

Tim caught Ivy's eye. "It's a very good idea."

She stiffened. "I know what you're thinking and I'm not moving out. Whoever this is, is after Cyril like you said."

His voice dropped to a whisper. "Suppose this person finds out Cyril talked to you and assumes he passed the item in question along."

For a moment she replayed the fear she'd felt the night Cyril had surprised her in the hallway. It would be comforting to let Tim take her away, keep her safe, feel his strong arms around her. She thought about how she'd let her guard down with Antonio, let him see her weaknesses. *No way, Ivy. You're tougher than that.* "I'll be fine here. I'm staying."

"And you say my principles are maddening."

Ivy and Tim went to her apartment and she made them both

some decaf coffee. Ivy added two sugars and a hefty dose of cream to hers. "Have you been able to find anything on Cyril?"

Tim took a sip of coffee. "Not much so far. He's lived in many different states. He bought the house here about six years ago. I can't find much of an employment history on him." His face was rueful. "I can tell you he applied for a fishing license recently."

She shook her head. "Can't see how that sheds any light on things."

"A friend of mine from church has a P.I.'s license so he can do more in-depth digging than I can. He said he'd look into it."

The bruise on Tim's face stood out sharply in the lamplight. She wondered again who had given it to him. Traces of fatigue lined his face. She was about to ask him a question when Madge poked her head through the open doorway.

"We're all packed up. Can Moe stay here with you for a minute while I bring the car around front?"

"Sure." Ivy opened the door fully and Moe stepped hesitantly inside. He stood just inside the doorway, next to his suitcase, clenching and unclenching his fists. Madge gave him a pat and went downstairs.

"Do you want to sit down, Moe?" Tim gestured to the chair next to him. "Why don't you relax for a minute?"

Moe fixed his gaze on the spindly ficus plant perched on the mantel. His lips moved but the words were inaudible.

Ivy took a step or two toward him, being sure not to crowd. "It's okay, Moe. We'll get your place fixed up again and the police will catch whoever did it."

Moe blinked rapidly. "M4e2d7s9c3i6z5t5r472cla0n7noe-6r5y9r9o7w2."

Tim stood. "What did you say, Moe?"

He repeated the cryptic string of numbers and letters, speaking more and more rapidly until the words were lost in the jumble of sound.

She shot a look at Tim. "What is he talking about?"

"I have no idea," he whispered back.

Ivy tried to catch Moe's eye. "We don't understand, Moe. Can you tell us what you mean?"

Moe didn't answer. His lips moved in a silent stream.

Madge rejoined them, car keys in hand. "All set. Let's go, honey. I'll make you some popcorn before bed. The Jiffy Pop kind for a special treat."

Moe closed his mouth and scurried into the hallway.

"Madge, Moe was saying something we couldn't understand. A bunch of letters and numbers. Do you know what he meant?"

"No, I never do. He's sort of got a gift for numbers. They comfort him, almost." She pushed a clump of graying hair out of her face. "I gave up trying to understand my son a long time ago. I just love him instead. It's the best I can do."

Tim grabbed the suitcase and followed Madge and Moe to the car.

Ivy watched from the window as they loaded up and Madge drove away.

When Tim rejoined her he was followed by Detective Greenly, who accepted her offer of coffee. He drained it in a few minutes and she refilled the mug. *So that's how police work gets done. It's fueled by coffee.* She felt a pain deep inside when she thought of her crew gathered around the morning coffeepot after a busy night, praying for a few hours of quiet.

Would she ever get back that family? That passion that burned inside of her? Would she feel again the sense of belonging and value? She looked over at Tim and his strong profile eased her discomfort.

"I've closed the apartment until we check for prints," Detective Greenly was saying.

Ivy snapped back to the present. "The break-in has to be related to Cyril's disappearance."

"No doubt." Greenly took another slug of coffee. He scrutinized Tim's face. "That's a pretty good shiner. What happened, son?"

"Nothing serious."

Greenly gave him a long look before he continued. "Have you

had any revelations about what Cyril might have given Moe? I couldn't get diddly out of the kid, and neither could his mother."

Ivy toyed with her coffee cup. "No. I can't think of anything. Money maybe? Did Cyril have access to money from somewhere?"

Greenly shook his head. "He was strictly small-time. Had a few payoffs at the track, tried some two-bit scam stuff. He worked at a package and mailing company for a while but got canned for pilfering items from the shipments. If he did come into some money, chances are it belonged to someone else who wants it back."

Tim nodded. "What can we do to keep Moe safe?"

"We'll handle it. Moving him from here is a big step. His mom lives in one of those complexes for active seniors. It's a busy place. Hard to get to him there without being seen. We've put the staff on alert to contact us if any strangers show up."

Ivy had been on many calls to Sunshine Corners, and the place was always buzzing with activities from the traditional bingo games to fencing classes. Moe would be well supervised there. She had a feeling Madge would be keeping close tabs on him as well.

Greenly put down his mug with a sigh. "Thanks for the coffee. I've got to go." He bobbed his chin at Tim. "Take care of that eye. Wouldn't want you to collect any more bruises."

Tim didn't answer.

Greenly narrowed his eyes for a moment, as if he was weighing his options. He tamped down his mustache. "Whatever is going on around here is a high-stakes game. It would be a good idea for both of you to play it safe for a while."

"Detective," Ivy said, "do you think something has happened to Cyril?"

He stretched his thick neck to work out a kink. "Don't know, but it's not a good sign about the plane ticket."

Tim's eyes widened. "What plane ticket?"

"It seems Cyril had a ticket on the red-eye last night. A one-way ticket to Mexico."

Goose bumps popped out on Ivy's arms. "But he never made it?"

The detective's look gave her the chilling answer.

TEN

Ivy dutifully showed up for her physical therapy appointment. She'd do anything to get a step closer to returning to work.

The physical therapist prodded Ivy's shoulder.

She tried not to grimace. "See? It's fine."

"I don't think we'd better start on any rehab for another few weeks. You're still in too much pain." The therapist clicked open a pen and jotted some notes in the file.

"It's not that bad. I did some bicep curls yesterday. I think I'm ready."

The woman looked at Ivy over the top of her glasses. "I know you're anxious to get back to work, but pushing yourself before the bone is mended is not the way to do it. You may mess things up to the point where you require surgery and then you'll be out for an even longer time."

"But…"

"A good rule of thumb for a clavicle injury is if it hurts, don't do it. Whether you want to admit it or not, you're hurting, so I'm not going to make your injuries worse by pushing too fast."

"It's not…"

"I appreciate your input, Ivy, but I'm the therapist here so why don't you let me do my job." She tucked the file under her arm. "Go see your M.D. to check the burns. Come back in a month. Keep it still with the figure-of-eight strap for a couple of days and don't exercise it. If it's feeling better by Thursday you can remove the strap for short periods. See you soon."

Ivy shrugged her clothes on, trying not to grumble too loudly. A few more weeks? With Wonder Woman Williams making herself indispensible to Captain Strong? No way.

She stalked out of the office and into the rapidly warming Tuesday afternoon. Gloom seemed to cover her in a tarry skin, sticking close as she strolled down the main street. The door to Corner Street Bookstore was open, the enticing scent of coffee perfuming the street outside. The sight of the bookstore reminded her of a question she needed to ask. Ivy went in.

Mr. Evans looked up from his pile of papers. "Hello, Ivy. Back so soon? What did you think of the books you bought last time?"

She flushed. "Actually, I haven't read them yet. I wondered about Cyril. Did you ever see him hanging out with Moe? Or anyone else?"

He smiled. "The police wondered the same thing. Sorry to say, since the day I refused to hire him I don't believe I saw him at all. Are you making any progress trying to locate him?"

"No." Her body felt drained. "Thanks, anyway. I guess I'll just browse while I'm here." Really, she just wanted to lose herself in the dark shadows and dusty corners of the store.

"Is the shoulder mending well?"

She sighed. "Not as quickly as I want it to." She headed for the far corner of the store where Mr. Evans kept a mishmash books.

She grabbed a couple and sat down on a scarred wooden chair by the window to thumb through some worn copies and try to think of something she'd missed. She looked out the tiny window to see her cousin Mitch coming out from the shop across the street. Charlie followed a few steps behind. Crouching on her knees to get a better look, she watched them talk.

Quickly she replaced the books and waved to Mr. Evans as she darted out into the street. Mitch was just firing up the engine of his motorcycle.

She hollered at him over the noise.

He didn't look up.

"Mitch," she yelled again, putting a hand on his arm.

He jerked, eyes wide. "Oh, hi, Ivy," he called. "Sorry, can't talk. Gotta take off."

"Stop running away from me. I need to talk to you."

"See you later, V." He waved and drove off down the street.

She turned to Charlie. "Do you know where he's going?"

He pushed back the brim of his cowboy hat. "No, ma'am. He doesn't clear his calendar with me."

"How was your fishing trip?"

"What fishing trip?"

"I thought you and Mitch went fishing."

"No, ma'am. I'd love to drop a line, but I've been plenty busy."

A car with fire department markings pulled up in the spot Mitch's motorcycle had just vacated.

Tim jingled his keys. "Perfect timing. Hey, Charlie. How are you?"

"Doing well. Off to pick up my Porsche. I love that car but it sure keeps my mechanic in business."

He tipped his hat again and headed away.

Tim turned to her. "How about lunch? My treat."

"I'm not feeling up to it."

"Okay. How about you keep me company while I eat and I'll tell you what I learned about Cyril?"

Her heart skipped a beat. "Something that might help?"

"Maybe. Sit with me and find out."

Ivy staked out a shaded table on the sidewalk while Tim went inside the small café. He came out with two falafels and sodas. "I thought you might be hungry later."

In spite of her dark mood, her mouth watered at the smell of spicy chickpeas inside the soft pita. She took a bite of the savory sandwich just as a fire engine roared down the street, sirens blasting.

She half rose, the instinct to respond overwhelming her senses. Jeff rode in the front, earphones in place, eyes intense. Denise sat in the backseat, leaning forward, eagerness painted all over her young face. In the next second they were gone, leaving behind only a wake of exhaust.

Ivy sagged back into the chair, tears welling up in the corners of her eyes.

Tim reached out a hand to cover hers. "Give it time, Ivy."

She snatched her hand away. "Time? I don't have time. You don't understand."

"Sure, I do. You're angry and frustrated that you can't work."

"It's not just about work. I feel like, like I've been pulled away from my family."

He took a sip of soda before he spoke. "I know about the brotherhood and all that, Ivy, but you have a family and people that love you, no matter what you do." An edge crept into his voice. "Even when you shut them out."

"So I'm committed to my job, Tim. That's not a crime." She tried to keep her voice level. "When Sadie died, I promised myself that I wouldn't let that happen to another soul if I could prevent it."

"And you haven't. You've saved lives and property. You've made a difference to a lot of people, but my point is that you are still a worthy, well-loved person even when you're not wearing your turnouts." His voice rose in volume. "And I could also add there are people, great people, heroic people all over the place who just don't happen to ride a fire engine for a living."

She bridled. "Well, I'm one of the lucky people who does."

"God made you Ivy Beria, not Firefighter Ivy Beria."

She balled up her paper napkin. "God doesn't factor into my life or my choices."

"Yes, He does, Ivy, whether you admit it or not."

She wanted to shake him, to throw her soda in his face and walk away. The rage swirled inside until she felt lost in it. She squeezed her eyes shut tight and tried to take deep breaths. When she opened them again, his eyes were locked on her face.

"I know it's hard. I'm sorry. I wish I could make it easier for you."

She wanted to be angry, but something in his face wouldn't let her. The anger drained away, leaving only a sorrow behind, a sorrow that felt as though it had started fifteen years ago, the day that her sister burned to death. It had dissipated for a while, lost in the fun she had with Antonio. But that was all it had been, fun.

Not love. Love was the kind of person who wanted all of you, the dark stuff, too.

A question leaped into her mind. Was that who Tim was? Someone who could love all of her? No, she didn't have the courage to find out. She blinked hard, swallowing the new tears that threatened. "What did you learn about Cyril?"

He continued to look into her eyes for a moment before he leaned back in the chair. "Cyril is a jack-of-all-trades, it seems."

"Meaning?"

"In addition to his recycling job, I found out he was a part-time electrician, did a few odd jobs around town."

"Okay."

"He worked on the old Oak Grove Hotel before the owners gave up on it."

"That empty building at the edge of town?" The place was a magnet for teen troublemakers until the city boarded it up tight.

"Uh-huh."

"I'll bite. What does this tell us about the guy?"

"I spoke to the building superintendent that was in charge of the project before it went belly-up. He hired Cyril and ultimately let him go but not because the money ran out."

She felt a tingle. "Then why did he fire Cyril?"

Tim gave her a satisfied smile. "The super's name is Chuck. He's a real nice guy. Met him at a church retreat a while back. He told me he had decided to get rid of Cyril anyway because he had a key made to the place and was using it for a second home, hosting poker nights there, sleeping over, even brought in a warming plate and cooler."

"And Chuck didn't tell the police that?"

"He didn't want to smear Cyril's reputation so he just left it that Cyril was sacked when the project folded."

Ivy's thoughts whirled. "So you think maybe Cyril is holing up at the Oak Grove Hotel?"

He shrugged. "I figure it's worth a look. I'm off the clock in an hour. We can take a drive over there and if anything looks out of order, we'll call Greenly."

She shook her head. "Tim, you are amazing. Why are you doing all this for me?"

He stroked her hand with his fingers. "I think deep down you know why."

She held his gaze for a moment, staring into those warm blue eyes. "I wish I could be the person that you want and deserve, Tim, but I can't." *I don't want to share myself with anyone, even a wonderful man like you.*

His smile was sad.

For the briefest of moments she wanted to move closer, share some of the peace that he radiated, let herself get lost in his sweet soul. Instead she pulled her hand away. "I'll see you in an hour then."

He sighed. "Okay. An hour."

Though Tim did his best to avoid the potholes, the road was bumpy and uneven.

It was three o'clock with temperatures close to ninety. Tim could understand why the hotel idea had appeal. The Oak Grove Hotel would really have been the perfect spot for a quiet getaway. The road that led up to it hadn't been paved so the tires had only gravel for traction as they climbed the steep, tree-lined slope. The lush green canopy bathed the trail in a delicious coolness. The scent of eucalyptus drifted through the open car window.

He wrestled the steering wheel as they rattled across a hole. "Sorry, Ivy. Is it hard on your shoulder?"

"No," she said, sounding as though she was gritting her teeth.

Tim concentrated on the structure that came into view around the last curve. It was a two-story, wood-frame building. The wide spaces where the picture windows should be were boarded up. A once-grand half-circle drive was sprinkled with weeds and the front veranda littered with broken pieces of wood and plaster. The whole lot was home to sprawling shrubs and clusters of thistle.

"Too bad." Tim shook his head. "It must have been a really fine hotel in its day." He parked a good distance from the structure, under the concealing branches of a massive oak. "I don't see any cars around, but I'm not sure Cyril owns one anyway."

They watched for several minutes, the only sign of movement coming from a squirrel that darted across the old shingled roof.

"We should take a look while we're here."

Tim nodded. "I think we might be able to see through the slats in the side window there." He leaned across her and pointed, trying to ignore the sweet smell of her shampoo.

They picked their way quietly over the rocky ground.

A crow squawked his displeasure at being disturbed. He flapped away with a rush of heavy wings.

Tim stepped up on the wooden porch and helped Ivy up behind him. He whispered in her ear. "Hang on a second. I think I can see through that gap if I get a little higher."

He climbed onto a stack of cracked red bricks that he surmised had been intended to trim the chimney. He hoisted himself up to the edge of a boarded-up window.

As his fingers cleared the edge, the pile shifted.

He fell with a loud crash.

ELEVEN

Nick started at the sound of a crash outside. Through the crack in the upstairs shutter he could see the man with the still-bruised eye lying in a pile of bricks and the girl firefighter talking quietly to him.

Nick let go of Cyril's neck with a disgusted sigh as he took a breath to control his rage. Cyril had made the mistake of angering Nick with his refusal to provide the goods. Anger wasn't a good thing in Nick's line of work, as Cyril's snapped neck proved. His boss wasn't going to like it. Cyril dead and still no merchandise recovered. He'd already searched the hotel from top to bottom before the scrawny man showed up, so he knew it wasn't there. Cyril had come in with a backpack, probably left it in the downstairs mess. It was unlikely, but it bore checking out.

Nick crept downstairs, avoiding the squeaky floorboards he'd noted on his way up earlier. The two outside seemed to be talking. He made it to the main floor before he saw the handle turn. He'd just enough time to snatch the backpack and squeeze back out through the loose shutter before they entered.

Holding the backpack and keeping his head down, Nick retreated, vanishing into the leafy screen where he'd hidden his motorbike. Once again, he settled down to watch and wait.

Ivy barely avoided the tumbling bricks. She scrambled over to where Tim lay on his back. "Are you okay?"

He blinked. "Yeah. Got a few more bruises to go with my eye, but nothing serious."

She brushed a cobweb off his cheek. "And you say I'm a trouble magnet." Her joke didn't elicit a smile. Instead he sat up and grabbed his cell phone.

"Who are you calling?"

"Detective Greenly." His forehead creased into a frown. "I saw a red backpack in there before I fell."

Ivy inhaled sharply, all her senses on fire. "Cyril."

He nodded. After a moment he hung up with a frown. "He's not in the office. The dispatcher is going to contact him and route him here."

Ivy chewed her lip. "Cyril will run as soon as he catches sight of a police car. Maybe we should try to talk to him first."

"Greenly won't like it."

She exhaled loudly. "If we wait for Greenly, we may never find out who is after Cyril."

"And Moe."

"And Moe," she agreed. After a silent decision, they crept to the door and turned the handle. It gave with only a small squeak of protest.

Tim scanned the room wildly. "I think he heard us. The red backpack I saw earlier is gone."

"Maybe he's hiding." She made a circle. The room was cluttered with construction debris, coated with dust and grime, but several clean patches on the floor hinted at recent activity. "Cyril?" she called. "It's Ivy. I'm Moe's friend. We need to talk to you."

The quiet was broken only by the sound of their breathing.

Tim pointed at the stairs. "Let's try up there."

Ivy trailed him up the steps, their combined weight making the wood groan in protest. The hallway opened up onto a series of rooms, ten in all. All of the doors were open. Tim poked his head into the first one. Ivy continued onto the second door.

She saw only the feet before the adrenaline took over. She immediately yelled for Tim as she ran to Cyril and checked his airway and pulse. By the time Tim careened into the room, Ivy had started compressions.

Tim carried on her efforts to find a pulse. "I think his neck is broken."

He took over the compressions while Ivy called it in.

They continued, alternating breathing and compressions, until it was clear there was no more life left in Cyril Donovan.

Ivy sat back, wiping the sweat from her forehead.

Tim groaned. "Oh, man. Is it possible he fell from something?"

"I don't think so." She'd seen plenty of death in her time with the fire department, but she'd never been so close to someone who'd just had their life taken in such a brutal manner. It sickened her, the colossal waste of a life, the cruelty of a powerful person over a weaker one. She held Cyril's hand for a moment. "I'm so sorry," she whispered. "So sorry."

Tim reached out a hand to her shoulder. "We should wait outside so we don't disturb any more evidence."

"No. I'm not leaving him alone here."

Tim didn't answer. Instead he sat down on the floor next to her, settling into the dust that swirled around the three of them.

They stayed another half hour before Detective Greenly arrived. His face was impassive, but his voice betrayed anger. "You should have waited for me."

Tim nodded. "Probably, but we weren't sure he was here at first. It could have been a wild-goose chase."

When the coroner arrived to take Cyril's body, Ivy stood, her knees cramped and shoulder aching. She stared at the space where he'd lain, alone. Cold waves seized her again.

Greenly walked them both downstairs, into the hot afternoon. "I was at the airport, doing some beating of the bushes. Seems Cyril did show up for his flight, but something spooked him and he took off just as the passengers started to board."

Tim shook his head. "Too bad he couldn't have made that flight."

"Yeah. We wouldn't be standing here right now." Greenly listened to Tim's recounting about the backpack again.

"Either he hid the thing somewhere after you spotted him or…" He stared at the ruined building jutting out against the blue sky.

It took a moment for the implication to sink into Ivy's brain. "Or whoever murdered him took it." For the first time she realized that the person who had choked the life out of Cyril might have been in the house at the same time they were.

She shivered, feeling the fear grip her insides.

Tim put an arm around her. "Are you done with us, Detective?"

"Sure, for now. By the way," he added, "I'd watch my back if I were you."

Ivy tried not to let the fear show as they walked back to the car.

Nick had taken the precaution of dismantling the backpack down to its nylon lining. Nothing. A pack of cards, a few dollars, a wadded-up sweatshirt and three candy bars. If he hadn't killed the guy, Cyril would have talked eventually. They all did. Nick allowed himself a moment of self-recrimination. Then he returned to practical matters. The merchandise was probably gone anyway, reduced to ashes in the house fire. He knew the probability would not be enough to satisfy his boss.

Now he eased open the door and waited to face the music.

His boss stood at the workbench, the vise holding the specimen in place while he pushed the glass eyes into the face. The area around the shiny orbs was bare of feathers, leaving the duck with an eerie expression of wide-eyed panic as if he were trying to fly off the table.

"What do you think?" He moved aside so Nick could get the full effect.

Try as he might Nick could never see the sense in killing something and then taking painstaking efforts to make it look alive again. Dead was dead. He kept these opinions to himself.

"Cyril is dead."

"How?"

"I was convincing him to tell me, and he refused. I lost control."

"Unfortunate. Did the girl see you?"

"No."

"Good. One dead body is enough trouble for now. The police are too close to my operations. I don't want to risk any more exposure."

Nick waited patiently. He knew it was not over.

The man's tone was mild. "I am disappointed. I expected my property to be returned to me by now."

"It probably burned up."

"Perhaps."

"Or he might have given it to someone. The kid, maybe. Or the girl."

"Find Moe then, but don't kill him unless you have to. You'll have to put pressure on the girl, too."

"I think she knows I'm watching her."

"Yes. Maybe we'll have to enlist someone to help you."

Nick frowned and made to leave. "Who?"

"Someone close to her, someone who has good reason to cooperate. And, Nick…" He punched the eye into the duck's head with an audible snap. "Let's get this matter tidied up quickly, shall we?"

Tim drove Ivy back to her apartment, lost in thought. He could not shake the shock of finding Cyril dead. It was such a waste. He breathed a prayer and tried to shift his mind to another topic. "I keep thinking about that string of letters and numbers that Moe rattled off. I wonder if it's somehow connected to whatever Cyril was hiding."

"It sounded like random talk to me."

"No, not random. He repeated it a couple times. His mother said he remembers things in sequence."

"I don't even recall what the string was."

He pulled out his PDA and repeated Moe's strange phrase. He took in her surprise. "I thought it might come in handy later."

"Sometimes you scare me with that left-brain thing. Could it be some phone numbers?"

"Too many digits, and the letters don't fit as names or addresses."

"I can't understand any of it. The whole thing is awful."

His heart ached at the defeat painted on her face. "You look tired. Are you going to be okay here tonight?"

The conversation was interrupted when Ivy's phone trilled. She answered it, and he could see a flush creep over her face. "Oh, hi. I'm busy right now."

Tim tried not to listen, noting that she retreated to a far corner of her apartment to finish the conversation. Her occasional laugh sounded high-pitched, nervous. When she hung up, he bit down on the question that burned inside him. She volunteered the information instead.

"That was Antonio."

Tim's stomach clenched. "Oh. Signing up to help with the search?"

"No, he, er, wanted to ask me something."

Tim took a deep breath and tried to keep his voice neutral. "Ivy, is Antonio looking to get back together with you?"

Her cheeks became infused with a deep pink. "I don't know. He just misses the fun we had, I think."

And do you want to go back to him? After he treated you like that? Tim wanted to scream the question along with some other choice remarks. Instead he cleared his throat. "Well, I guess I'd better be going. You sure you don't want to go stay with your mom?"

"Yes, I'm sure. I'll lock the door, I promise. Greenly said he's going to come check the apartment grounds after he's done at the hotel."

"I'm not convinced. I think…"

"Go, Tim."

He read her determined expression and knew he wasn't going to change her mind. He made a plan of his own. "All right." He checked his watch. "Call me if you need anything."

"Okay." She walked him to the door. "Tim? It was some really good investigation work to find Cyril."

Though her comment pleased him, he could not summon up a smile. "I just wish I could have found him a few minutes sooner."

* * *

Ivy heard a knock early the next morning.

She pulled on her ratty blue bathrobe and tiptoed to the door, squinting through the peephole.

Ivy yanked open the door. "Mitch?"

Her cousin looked tired, his dark eyes smudged underneath with shadows. "Hey, V. Did I wake you up?"

She looked at the clock. In truth she'd been awake, thinking about Moe and Cyril. "It's seven thirty. That's a little early for you, isn't it?"

He shrugged. "I have an early shift today." He walked into the small kitchenette and began to make a pot of coffee.

In spite of the hour, she was glad to see him. The night before had been so strange with her unfounded fear at her mother's house and Antonio's cheerful call. It was comforting to see her cousin's familiar face. "So what brings you here? You're not one to drop by unless there's pizza."

"What? Can't I stop and check in on my favorite cousin? How's the shoulder?"

"Sore."

"Heard you found a dead guy yesterday."

She shivered. "News travels fast."

"Small town. You okay?"

"I guess so."

He returned to the living room with two cups of coffee. "Weird that it was the guy who owned the house that collapsed on you. I guess what goes around comes around."

She arched an eyebrow. "Why do you say that? Mitch, did you know Cyril?"

"Know him? Nah, not really. Ran into him a few times, I guess. I think he showed up at Charlie's once while I was over there. Knocked on the door, offered to do some landscaping work."

"Really? Did Charlie hire him?"

"Nah." Mitch laughed. "You've seen Charlie's place. The gardens are picture-perfect, not a leaf out of place. Anyway, I actually came by to ask you a favor."

"What favor?"

"Well, since you aren't supposed to be driving and all that, can I borrow your car? I've got a class in Portland tomorrow and I need some wheels."

"Why don't you take your bike?"

"Uh, I decided to sell it."

Her mouth fell open. "You sold your motorcycle? You love that thing."

He shrugged before taking a gulp of coffee. "No biggie. It needed some work done so I figured I'd unload it and buy something else, but I haven't decided what yet. Maybe the Mercedes Charlie's thinking of selling." He ran a hand through his hair.

She looked at his tanned wrist. "Where's your watch?" He'd made a point of showing off his Swiss precision watch to her when he'd bought it a few months ago.

"Must have forgotten to put it on."

She put down her coffee and rounded on him. "Come on, Mitch. I'm not a fool. What is going on here? You sold your bike. You've been moody and irritable. What gives?"

His eyes flashed. "Nothing. I just came over here to borrow your car. If I wanted the third degree I could have gone home to my mother."

"You're my cousin and I care about you, so don't bother with the indignation." She tossed him the keys. "Take the car but at least tell me the truth. What is going on?"

He grabbed the keys and shot out of the sofa. "Nothing is going on, Ivy, and I wish you and everybody else would just leave me alone." He slammed the door so hard a picture fell off the wall and crashed to the floor.

Before the echo died away it came to her.

She had a feeling she knew who had given Tim the black eye.

TWELVE

Ivy fixed Tim with a hard stare until he started to squirm. "Well? Are you going to tell me why Mitch punched you or not?"

"If you want to know, let's go talk to him right now." Tim grabbed his keys. "I'm off work and we might as well get this over with."

"Why didn't you tell me he hit you?"

"Because you'd want to know why."

"I do want to know why."

"Exactly."

Tim remained infuriatingly silent as they drove across town. She knew by the hard set of his jaw that he wasn't going to be badgered into telling her anything. He could be as stubborn as she. They pulled up at Mitch's condo a few minutes after eleven.

The sound of breaking glass sent them running toward his front door. Ivy slammed the door open in time to see a dark-haired stranger whack Mitch's head against the carpeted floor. She recognized the mob guy from the photo Greenly had shown them. Tim launched himself at the man and got him around the knees. He fell with a crash that shook the floor.

"Stop," Mitch said.

Ivy dove on the man's back to try to secure his hands. The three of them went around in a messy tangle of arms and legs. Ivy tried to hold on to the stranger's ankles but he jerked away, kicking her in the shoulder.

She cried out in pain.

With a surge of strength the black-haired man shoved Tim

away and ran toward the door. Tim scrambled to his feet to follow, but Mitch's voice stopped them.

"Let him go." Mitch struggled to his feet and flopped into a chair. "He won't come back."

Tim helped Ivy up and they stood there, panting, staring at Mitch.

He slouched in the chair, one hand pressed to the bump on his head, hair in disarray, shirt torn.

"Who is he?" Ivy managed at last. "Tell me what is going on here right now or I'm calling the cops."

Mitch waved them onto the sofa. "He's with some people in New York. Some people I borrowed money from."

Ivy tried to find a comfortable position for her aching shoulder and steady her breathing. "Money for what?"

"To cover some debts."

"What debts? You have a good job. Why did you need to borrow from a loan shark?"

He blinked and looked away.

Tim stared at the floor. "You need to tell her, man, or I will. I'm not going to lie to her."

Mitch pressed his lips together.

Tim cleared his throat. "He's been gambling, online."

Ivy gasped. "What? Why? You have so many friends, so many social things. Why would you do that?"

"Aww, it's no big thing, Ivy. A few of my buddies got me into online poker. It was just something new to do, at first, a way to pass the time. Then, well—" his gaze traveled to the floor "—I sorta got hooked on it."

"How much do you owe, Mitch?"

"I'm not sure."

She glowered at him. "Ballpark it for me."

"Fifty thousand."

Her gasp was loud in the still room. "You owe that guy fifty thousand dollars? Oh, Mitch."

"Not anymore. I paid him off. He won't be back. He just roughed me up a little to teach me a lesson."

She folded her arms. "And just where did you get your hands on fifty thousand dollars?"

"I sold my watch and my bike." His eyes were dull with sadness. "And I went to, um, a friend to borrow the rest. He said he'd give me time to pay it back."

Ivy grimaced. "What friend?"

"It doesn't matter. It's done now."

"It's not going to be done until you've paid it all back and quit gambling."

Mitch snorted. "Well, your pal here took care of that."

Ivy looked at Tim, whose cheeks pinked in little-boy fashion.

"I, er, sort of confiscated his computer."

She looked at the desk, which was empty now, save the printer.

"I told him I'd give it back when he started attending some Gamblers Anonymous meetings or seeing a counselor, pastor, something." Tim looked closely at Mitch. "It's not a complete fix, is it? I mean, people can get online in many different ways. Have you been keeping away from it?"

Mitch leaped out of the chair. "Yes, Mother, I have. And don't you have anything else to do besides manage my life? Both of you?"

Tim smiled. "Not until you beat this thing."

"Well, thanks for the help, but I'm over it. The New York people are paid off and I've got time to work on the other. I'm on track, guys, so you can just back off now."

Tim cocked his head. "And this friend. He loaned you the money with no strings attached?"

Mitch glared at him. "Yes. Look, I'm done talking about it with both of you. Thanks for stopping by and all, but I'd really like you to leave."

Ivy walked to the door in a state of shock. She'd barely followed Tim across the threshold when Mitch slammed the door behind them.

She turned on him. "I can't believe it. How long have you known?"

Tim rubbed his face. "Not long. I knew something was going

wrong with him, but I didn't know for sure until I showed up on his doorstep one night and he was playing poker online. Then he started acting strange, missing get-togethers, backing out on things. He asked me to borrow money a few months back. He said it was for an investment. I think it was actually to cover some bills. When Greenly showed us the picture of the goon, I realized I'd seen him talking to Mitch a few days before. I put two and two together."

Ivy tried to sort out the cacophony of feelings that raced through her. Mitch was a gambler, on the brink of financial ruin. And Tim had known all about it. "You should have told me."

He sighed. "Maybe. I tried to help him the best way I could think of."

"He's my family and I should be the one taking care of him."

"No," he said, eyes burning. "You can't save everyone, Ivy. Only God can do that."

"That's not true. He doesn't save them. He lets people die and that's why I do what I do."

She could remember every second of the horror, the car that cut them off, the dizzy feeling as their truck flipped, skidding on its side until it crashed into the center divider. The flames that erupted from the engine. Ivy managed to crawl out through the passenger window, but her sister was jammed against the driver-side door.

She could still here Sadie's voice, cracked and hoarse with pain. "Go get help."

"I don't want to leave you."

"Go," Sadie had said, her eyes half closed. "It will be all right."

But it wasn't. As soon as Ivy cleared the window, the blaze grew, engulfing the car. Then the whole thing was aflame. And Sadie was gone.

She felt the anger as though it had happened only moments ago.

Tim was holding out his hand to her. "Life or death is not up to you, Ivy. You don't always get to be the hero."

She could not speak. Grief filled up her throat. "You are cruel."

He took a step toward her. "I don't mean to be, Ivy. I just want you to see how heavy the burden is you're carrying. You're so busy trying to save lives you aren't living your own. I want to help you. I…"

Her whisper was fierce. "Don't help me. Don't do anything for me. Leave me alone." She spun on her heel and left him there, arms slightly raised as if he meant to embrace her.

"At least let me drive you home," he called.

"I can get home myself." She stalked down the sidewalk.

Tim was arrogant and judgmental. Self-righteous was more like it, telling her how she wasn't living her life right. Right with whom? With God? Why should she try to make it right with Him? After what He'd done to Sadie.

Why had Ivy gotten out when her sister had not? Why hadn't the glass given under the weight of Ivy's frantic hands as she tried to free her sister?

And why hadn't the firefighters been able to get there before the flames engulfed the truck in a white-hot inferno? Her fingers balled into fists. Maybe Tim was right. She was carrying around a burden since her sister died, but so what? So what if she made it her mission to save people when God wouldn't?

It wasn't Tim's place to judge, anyway. He was…what? The truth filled up her brain before she had a chance to screen it out. Closer than family. A bigger part of her life than she had realized before.

How had she let him in when she'd done such a thorough job of keeping everyone else out?

She exhaled sharply. It wouldn't happen again. The very moment, the second her shoulder healed up, Ivy would be back on the line, back where she belonged. And she would take care of Mitch herself, somehow. She was so lost in her thoughts it took two rings before she heard the cell phone beeping in her pocket.

"Hello?"

"Ivy? It's Madge. I'm sorry to bother you, but I need help. Please. Right away. Moe got so upset when I told him about Cyril he took off. Oh, please help me find him. I'm frantic."

Ivy calmed her as best she could. "I'll be there as soon as I can."

She didn't want to talk to Tim, let alone sit next to him, but she had to find Moe before he got hurt. With resignation, she dialed Tim's number. "Moe's disappeared. Mitch has my car. Can you pick me up?"

"Yes. I'll be there in sixty seconds."

"What? How…?"

"I'm only two blocks behind you."

She whirled around. Sure enough, there was Tim's truck approaching.

"Why are you following me?" she said as she got in.

He looked sheepish. "You were upset. I wanted to make sure you got home okay."

She wanted to be angry at him, to sustain the fury she'd felt at his earlier words, but the rueful expression on his face melted away her hostility. "I'm still upset."

"I know."

"And I don't want to talk about it."

"I figured as much."

"So let's just concentrate on finding Moe."

"Okay by me."

Madge had the door open when they drove up. She danced back and forth on her thick legs. "He was so upset. He just sort of screamed and shut himself in the bedroom. I figured he would be okay in there but then I realized it was really quiet. I checked on him, and the window was open. He's gone." Her breath came in pants, and an unhealthy paleness crept into her cheeks.

"Sit down," Ivy said, guiding her to a chair. "Tim and I will go look for him. He can't have gotten far. You stay here in case he returns."

She nodded, dashing the tears from her plump face.

Tim and Ivy went in separate directions down the quiet street, calling Moe's name. A half hour later they rendezvoused in the wooded lot behind the library.

"I didn't see him anywhere." Tim wiped the sweat from his forehead.

"Me, neither, but the librarian said she saw him running north through the trees."

"North? Where would he be headed in that direction?"

Their eyes met and they spoke at the same time. "The apartment."

They jogged back to Tim's truck and took off.

Twenty minutes later they'd arrived back at the complex.

The elevator took too long so they ran up the steps two at a time until they came to the sixth floor. Panting, they hammered on Moe's door.

"Moe, it's Ivy. Please open the door. Your mother sent us." She tried the knob only to find it locked.

Tim grabbed her arm.

"What?"

"Do you smell something?"

Ivy's eyes widened, amazed that she hadn't noticed it right away. The faint smell of smoke wafted out from under the door.

Ivy's actions became automatic. She ran to her own apartment and grabbed the spare key Madge had given her. On the way back she snatched the fire extinguisher from the wall. Tim held the extinguisher while she unlocked the door, and they both burst into the room.

Moe crouched on the living-room floor, watching the small pile of rubbish smolder. Flames burst forth between the gaps in the books, magazines and clothing he'd dumped there. He didn't look up at Tim or Ivy, just continued to stare at the tendrils of fire. A spark caught his pant leg and still he didn't move, even when it started to smolder.

Ivy manhandled him as gently as she could to the floor. "Cover your face with your hands, Moe," she called.

Amazingly, he did as she told him and she rolled him until the fire was out.

While she was treating Moe, Tim aimed the extinguisher at the base of the flames and set to work. Though the room was permeated with acrid fumes, it didn't take long for him to knock down the small fire.

Ivy moved Moe close to the door, grabbed a broom handle and spread the materials out to be sure the fire was finished. Tim opened the windows to help air out the smoke.

Moe began to rock back and forth. "It's got to go," he said. "It's got to go."

"What does, Moe?" Tim approached slowly, his tone soft and soothing. "Why were you burning these things?"

Ivy picked up a sodden sweater with a patch on the elbow. "I don't think I've ever seen Moe wear this kind of thing before." A thought occurred to her. "Moe, are these Cyril's things?"

Moe's eyes widened.

Tim exchanged a look with her. "Uh, it's okay, Moe. Really. It's okay, we'll just clean these things up and it will be fine."

Moe rocked forward on his heels. Before Ivy could stop him, he'd grabbed some foam-covered items from the sodden pile.

"Tim, don't let him…" It was too late. Moe bolted for the open door and vanished down the hallway.

"Wait a minute, Moe," Tim yelled as he took off in pursuit.

Ivy made sure the fire was completely out before she called Detective Greenly. When he was en route, she looked over the pile on the singed carpet: two journals called *Medical Horizons,* one about birds, and a mangled sweater. There was also a half-eaten box of crackers and what appeared to be an unopened pack of gum.

Was this odd collection really Cyril's? Why had he given it to Moe?

Cyril's words came back to her. *Tell him to take care of what I gave him.*

She poked at the mess with her toe, knowing Greenly would not appreciate her disturbing whatever evidence might be present.

Tim returned, panting, twenty minutes later. "He's gone. I couldn't catch him. He runs like an Olympic sprinter. I called Madge and alerted her." He flopped onto the love seat. "Man. This whole thing gets weirder all the time. Why did he set fire to this stuff?"

"I don't know. It just looks like a bunch of junk to me."

"Yeah." Tim surveyed the mess. "I wonder why the guy was reading medical journals, though. He didn't seem like the type."

She had no answer to give. "Moe looked terrified, poor guy. He doesn't understand what is going on here, either."

"What did he take from the pile before he ran?"

"I'm not sure. It was something small. I didn't get a good look." She paced the small room. "I'm worried about Moe. After we talk to Greenly do you want to help me search for him? If you don't mind playing rescue hero with me, that is."

Tim smiled. "There's nothing I'd rather do. And, Ivy, about what I said before…"

She held up a hand to stop him. "Let's talk about it later. Okay?"

He smiled. "Anytime, Ivy, anywhere."

She enjoyed the inexplicable hint of comfort that crept into her heart just before Greenly stepped in the door.

THIRTEEN

He could virtually smell the fear that crept through the phone line. Nick listened as his boss talked into the receiver.

"If you've finished, then? Your obligation is clear whether or not your conscience is. Unless you'd like to repay the hundred thousand with interest?"

Silence.

"I didn't think so. We have only a small wrinkle on this end, a delay that has briefly prevented our shipment. It will be resolved quickly. At that time you will supply the other piece of information."

The forced calm in his boss's voice did not fool Nick.

"Do you understand me, Roger?"

He waited a beat before he continued. "Very good. And Roger? Please do not contact me again. I abhor discussing business on the phone. Goodbye."

He watched as his boss hung up and made himself a cup of tea.

Nick sighed, feeling again the sting of humility because he had not been able to resolve things. A distant memory rose to the surface. He remembered his father's face when the men lifted their sticks. Heard him cry out for mercy. They didn't know it, but the brutes collecting their protection money at his father's small shop in New York decades ago had made him a man that day. He resolved in that white-hot moment that he would never be weak. What's more, he understood in that same moment that the real power was not in the big men with their clubs, but in the quiet, faceless man who sent them. He worked for just such a man now. A man who expected results.

Cyril's face swam before his. How had he been duped by a nobody? Chances are the stolen item would never be recovered and if it was, it would mean nothing to the finder. But that was a dangling thread in the fine cloth his boss had woven. A dangling thread that needed to be cut.

His boss looked up from his tea. He didn't speak, but Nick understood.

They searched everywhere they could think of, from the library to the comic book store and every square inch in between. Tim finally forced Ivy to join him on a bench along the main street as the sun blazed in the late afternoon sky.

Tim stretched his legs in front of him. Frustration piled on top of fatigue. "My feet are killing me."

Ivy yawned. "Mine, too. Where could Moe have gotten to? He didn't get that much of a head start and he doesn't drive. He must have holed up somewhere for the night."

They turned at the sound of a familiar voice. Mitch joined them on the bench.

Ivy stared at him. "Where did you come from?"

"I was doing some shopping." He picked at a spot of lint on his jeans. "So, um, well, I wanted to apologize. You know, for throwing you out of my place and all that. It was…"

"Terrible of you?" Tim helped.

"Yeah. Anyway, how about I make it up to you and buy dinner?"

Eyeing Ivy's reluctant expression, Tim shook his head. "Thanks anyway, but we've been on our feet for the past few hours. We're too tired to go out to eat."

"Did you find him?"

"Who?"

"The kid. That nutty kid who lives in your complex. Isn't that who you're looking for?"

"Yeah," Ivy said. "How did you know that?"

He shrugged. "We got a bulletin at work to keep our eyes peeled for him. I knew it had to be the kid you're always talking about. Come on, let's go get some food."

Tim struggled to his feet and held out a hand to Ivy.

She stood, shaking her head. "No, Mitch. The only thing I want now is a long bath."

"Okay. How about a coffee then?"

"Thanks, but I'll take a rain check."

Tim found his keys. "I'm going to drive her home. Maybe another time."

"Suit yourself." Mitch shuffled away.

Tim waited while Ivy buckled the seat belt carefully over her shoulder. He watched Mitch pull out his cell phone as he walked away. He wondered again who the faceless friend was supplying him with supposedly string-free money. He resolved to try keep an eye on Mitch if he could.

"Thinking about Mitch?"

Tim started. "Oh, yeah. Just wondering where he got that money."

"Me, too. I think I've got an idea. Can we make a stop on the way back?"

"Sure. Where to?"

"I think it's time to see Charlie."

Charlie? Tim's mind raced. Maybe to help out he'd loaned Mitch the money. He was the type who would do it, but something didn't feel right about the idea. He didn't comment as they drove toward Charlie's well-kept Victorian on the outskirts of town, stopping only long enough to grab a couple of sodas on the way.

Tim knocked on the heavy oak door.

Charlie answered their knock and invited them in.

They settled into leather chairs in a beautifully appointed parlor. Neatly stacked file folders lay on a polished cherry desk. A pair of glasses sat on top of the pile.

"So what brings you here?"

Ivy cut in before Tim could answer.

"I want to talk to you about Mitch."

"Sure. What about him?"

"You two are pretty close. You hang out together all the time."

"Yeah. We're good friends. We've worked together for more than five years now. He's an excellent flight nurse."

"So you'll understand why I'm asking. Did you know about his gambling?"

He blinked. "Gambling?"

Ivy nodded without looking away from Charlie's tanned face.

Groaning inwardly, Tim cleared his throat loudly. "What she meant to say is—"

Ivy cut in. "Yes, I said gambling."

"We play a few rounds of online poker sometimes, and blackjack."

"Still?"

"Still?" He raised one eyebrow, the faint white line of a scar cutting through it.

"You know what I mean. I can see in your face that you know Mitch has a gambling problem. Did you loan him money to pay off someone who was muscling him?"

"No." He put his cup down. "I wasn't aware he was in that kind of trouble. Mitch and I do things together for fun but I'm not married to him. His life is his own."

"And you're not helping his life by gambling with him. Is that how you afford this nice place, Charlie?"

"Ivy…" Tim started, but it was too late.

The easy smile vanished from Charlie's face. "I've been pleasant up to this point because you are Mitch's cousin, but I do not appreciate your accusations. Gambling is like a gun, Ivy. It's only bad when people misuse it." He stood up. "I think it would be a good idea if you left now."

Ivy stood and Tim followed her to the door. The door slammed as they went to the truck.

Tim stared at her, trying to keep his exasperation in check. A couple of deep breaths didn't help.

"What?"

"I wouldn't say that was brimming over with tact."

"Well, hasn't it occurred to you that Charlie might be the one who got Mitch into this mess?"

"Mitch got Mitch into this mess."

"You know what I mean."

Tim sighed. "It did make me wonder if he was the one who bailed Mitch out with the mob guys, but, Ivy, if we're wrong, would Mitch want the people he works with to know about his problem?"

"I'm sure Charlie already knew."

"Well, what if he didn't?" Tim gripped the steering wheel. "You're messing around with people's reputations here. In particular, a person who didn't want us involved in the first place."

"Then…" Ivy's voice trailed off. She groaned. "Oh, man. I shot my mouth off again, didn't I?"

"I wasn't going to put it like that, but, yes, you did." He reached out and took her hand, keeping his tone light. "Sometimes you batter down the door before you check to see if it's locked."

She gave him a wan smile. "You are very sweet to put it so gently. I'm an idiot."

"No, not an idiot. You just want to protect Mitch." He loved her for her unflinching desire to protect her family. He felt the same way about his own, only he included her on the list.

Her cell phone buzzed, startling them both. "It's a text message." He watched her face change as she read it. "It's from the chief. She wants to talk to me about my return date. She's going to let me come back."

Tim made himself smile, though he couldn't avoid the truth. When she returned to the line, he'd be lucky to see her ever. He forced a cheerful tone. "There, you see? I told you it would work out. When does she want to talk to you?"

"Right now."

"This late in the day?"

"We work twenty-four-hour shifts, remember? The fire department is never closed."

"Ah, yes. I forgot we aren't talking about mere mortals here." He put on his blinker and signaled a turn. "I assume your calendar is free to meet with her now?"

Ivy laughed. "I'd walk through fire to get there."

He felt a mixture of love and regret. "Somehow I can believe that."

They pulled up at the station a scant half hour later. Ivy inhaled deeply, the smell of chili on the stove mingled with the pungent scent of the floor cleaner. She wanted to wrap herself up in the joy of being back.

Jeff looked up from a binder he was studying. His face brightened and he hugged her. "Hi, Ivy. Great to see you. How's the shoulder?"

She wiggled her fingers and shrugged gently. "Better all the time."

Jeff shook Tim's hand. "Hey, man. Sorry the team lost."

"It happens. We'll get 'em next year."

Ivy peered down the hall. "Is Strong in her office?"

He nodded.

"I'll catch up with Jeff for a minute." Tim sat next to him at the table while Ivy went down the corridor to find the chief.

Strong sat in her office, going through reports, a pencil stuck behind her ear. She was so lost in concentration, Ivy had to knock twice on the open door.

"Oh, Ivy." She got up and gave her a soft hug. "How are you doing?"

"The doctor says I can start therapy after a few more weeks."

"Excellent. Glad to hear it."

Ivy fidgeted, drawing a deep breath before she started in. "I've been thinking about everything. I know that, um, sometimes I don't take the time to see the big picture before I charge in. I realize that's something I need to work on."

Strong's expression was slightly bemused. "Wow. Well, I'd have to agree with you there. I think it's something we can take a look at when we're ready to talk about your future with the department."

"Ready? I'm ready now. Isn't that why you asked me to come by?"

She frowned. "I didn't ask you to come by. Where did you get that idea?"

"The message. I got a text message from you asking me to stop by the station."

Strong shook her head. "I'm sorry, Ivy. I didn't send it. I know you're eager to come back, but there's really nothing to talk about until your doctor gives the all clear."

She felt as though she'd been socked in the gut. "You—you didn't leave the message?"

There was pity in the chief's eyes. "Sorry, must be some sort of mix-up."

Ivy tried to collect herself, her cheeks hot with embarrassment. "No, I'm sorry. I must have gotten my wires crossed." She stumbled to the door.

"It's good to see you, Beria."

Ivy could feel Strong's eyes on her as she escaped into the hallway.

Hardly registering what had happened, she walked slowly back out to the kitchen area. On her way she passed the workout room. Denise Williams waved as she worked the elliptical machine. Her face glistened with sweat. "Hello, Ivy. Great to see you up and around."

"Thanks." No wonder the woman looked happy. She was making steady progress toward taking Ivy's job away. Ivy gritted her teeth to keep from saying anything further. She continued on, leaving the able-bodied Denise to her vigorous workout. The injustice of it all almost choked her.

Tim and Jeff stopped talking when they saw Ivy.

Jeff's eyebrows shot up. "That was fast."

Feeling tears just below the surface, she couldn't face telling them what had happened. "Yeah. Quick and easy. I'm beat. Can you take me home now, Tim?"

His look was puzzled. "Sure."

"Don't you want to stay for some chili? It's Spinelli's day to cook. He promised his apple caramel nut pie later. You can't say no to that."

"Save me a slice." She hugged him and they escaped into the street.

She resisted Tim's gentle questions all the way back to the apartment. When he parked the truck, they sat in silence for a moment before they stepped out into the still evening.

Tim put an arm around her. "Ivy, whatever happened, I'm sorry. I know it upset you a lot. Is there anything I can do?"

She felt hot tears well up and course down her face. "It was all some kind of cruel trick. The chief didn't message me. She doesn't want to lay eyes on me until the doctor signs off."

Tim looked startled. "What?"

Ivy nodded miserably. "And I ran into Miss 'I'm as Healthy as an Ox' Williams. She's only too happy to take my job."

He folded her into his arms.

She snuggled deep into the warmth, comforted by the steady beat of his heart against her cheek. "It was humiliating."

"I'm so sorry, Ivy. It probably seemed a lot worse to you than it did to the chief."

When her gush of tears eased up, Tim wiped the moisture from her face with gentle fingers. His smile was tender. "You are so beautiful." He reached down and traced a finger over her lips.

Ivy was lost in a swirl of feeling, her stomach full of butterflies.

For a moment she embraced the sweetness, and it felt like the most natural thing in the world. Then the logic of the situation intruded and she pulled away with an effort. *Don't let yourself love him, Ivy. You've been hurt enough.* "I can't…"

He looked stricken. "I'm sorry. I apologize."

"Forget it. It's been a strange day." They continued walking, her heart still beating a loud staccato in her chest.

They made it a few more paces before he stopped short.

"What? What is it?"

"Nothing. I'm sure it's my imagination."

"Tell me."

"I was just thinking about the person who sent the message. What if they weren't trying to humiliate you?"

"What do you mean?"

"What if..." He looked up toward the sixth floor. "What if they were trying to get you away from here for some reason?"

Ivy looked from him to the building.

They ran.

FOURTEEN

Tim got there first. Her door was ajar. He motioned to her to stay put as he crept over the threshold. She waited as long as she could and then followed him.

The place was completely upended, in much the same way Moe's had been. Drawers emptied, the area rug rolled up along the edges, kitchen cabinets disgorged onto the floor. The radio was playing, no doubt to cover the sound of the intruder's actions. Without a word she went into her tiny bedroom and found a similar mess, her clothes closet and drawers dumped onto the carpet in colorful piles. She made her way to the closet.

A figure in a ski mask exploded from the closet and knocked her backward as she screamed. In spite of her shock, she managed to reach out and grab his ankles as he went past. The man fell with a crash, knocking over the pitcher on the bedside table. Ivy hung on to his ankle until a hard kick made her let go.

She heard a shout from the living room, followed by another crash. Ivy managed to get to her feet and stagger down the hallway to find Tim on the floor, struggling under the weight of an upended bookcase.

"Tim, are you all right?" She scooped books away from his flailing legs while he shoved the bookcase off and sat up.

"I'm okay." His eyes were frantic. "Are you?"

She gave him a shaky nod. "I think so. He was hiding in the closet."

He shook his head in disbelief. "I heard you scream and came running, but the guy managed to get by me and knock over the bookshelf. Who was he? Did he look familiar?"

"I'm not sure. He's stocky and strong, like the guy who tried to take my purse. I couldn't make out the hair color—did you?"

"No." He was silent for a moment. "Whoever it was is getting more desperate."

The whole thing seemed suddenly too much. Ivy turned away so Tim wouldn't see the tears forming in her eyes. "I'm going to see if anything was taken."

She returned to the bedroom.

With her breath in her throat she stepped into the closet and found her turnouts, lying in a pile, all the pockets inside out. She examined them from top to bottom, but they hadn't been damaged. Gathering them up, she pressed the yellow neoprene, still permeated with the faint smell of smoke, to her face.

Tim looked in cautiously. "Is your gear okay?"

"Yeah." She retrieved the boots and radio and put them in a neat pile in an empty closet corner. "At least I've still got that."

Detective Greenly came shortly. He wore jeans and a T-shirt and smelled like charcoal.

"Barbecue duty at my kid's high school. Some sort of wrestling team bonding thing, which ends with everybody sleeping on the gym floor tonight. Not me. I said I'd cook but leave the lying on the cold floor bit to the young bucks." He looked around. "Anything taken?"

"Not that I could tell." Ivy told him about the strange message she'd received before her humiliating trip to the fire station.

The detective's eyes rolled in thought. "Bad news is someone is still looking for whatever Cyril handed over. More bad news is he thinks you might be involved now."

Tim groaned. "What's the good news?"

"He hasn't found it yet. I'll dust for prints, but I'm not optimistic about that. You might want to find another place to stay for a bit until we get this cleared up." He turned his back on them and dialed his cell phone.

They didn't talk much. After Greenly left, it took hours to put the place back in semistraight order. During a break, Tim stuck his head in the refrigerator. "How about I whip us up some cheese omelets for dinner?"

She nodded, tackling another pile of scattered books.

He busied himself in the kitchen, finally sliding two puffy golden mounds onto plates.

"Heavenly Father," Tim said, taking her hand in his. "Thank You for this nourishment, and for keeping Ivy safe today."

She blinked. Keeping her safe? He'd let some nut into her apartment to ransack the place. She was in more danger now than she had been and still unemployed with no end in sight. This was God's idea of safe?

A thought startled her out of her self-pity. But here she was, safe from the intruder, and in spite of her jobless condition, she was sitting in her cozy apartment, eating a delicious meal with a man who'd spent the day shepherding her through one crisis after another. She looked at his head, bowed and humble, and something moved inside her. "Thanks," she blurted, her voice feeling rusty. "Thanks. Amen."

The smile he gave her when he looked up was nothing short of dazzling. She hastily started on her dinner. In spite of the evening's turmoil, Ivy found herself wolfing down the creamy eggs and cheddar. "You are a good cook."

"If you like omelets or anything barbecued, I'm your man." He gave her a meaningful look. "It wouldn't be a bad idea..."

"No." She put down her fork with a clang. "I know what you're going to say and nobody is forcing me out of my apartment. Nobody. We've covered this already."

"How did you know I was going to suggest that?"

"It's written all over your face."

He smiled. "So much for my steely detective demeanor. You're a stubborn gal, Ivy."

"That's what Sadie used to say, only not so nicely."

"Did you fight a lot?"

"Yeah. She was a terrible slob and I hated sharing a room with her." Ivy's voice trembled. "Now, I'd give anything to have her there, making a mess."

"I didn't know Sadie, but I think she probably is getting a big kick out of the situation right now."

"How so?"

He gestured around to the kitchen debris, which still lay piled all over the counter. "Doesn't look like the home of a neat freak to me."

She laughed and they set to work tidying until it was close to eleven o'clock. "Good enough," Ivy groaned. "I'm too tired to clean anymore."

"I was hoping you'd say that." He headed for the door. "Are you sure…"

"Yes, I'll be perfectly fine here. No running off because of strange text messages or anything. Doors and windows bolted. No strangers in the closet. Cell phone at the ready. Good night, Tim." She stopped him, fingering the button on his shirtfront. "Thank you so much for everything. I don't know what I did to deserve a…friend like you."

He leaned forward to kiss her and then stopped.

Her lips ached for his and for a split second she almost allowed herself to close the distance between them. Then she shook away the thought. *You're overwhelmed by the day. Things will be back to normal in the morning.*

"Good night, Ivy. Don't forget to lock up tight."

She shivered as he disappeared into the dark hallway.

I won't.

Though he hadn't the time to search as thoroughly as he wanted before they'd returned from the goose chase, he'd seen enough. She didn't have it, not in the apartment, anyway. He'd bet his new fishing rod on that.

Nick comforted himself with the notion that he had made significant progress, narrowing down the more likely target to the strange kid. If the girl didn't have it, then Moe had what he was looking for. Sooner or later, he'd catch up with him, but just to hedge his bets, he'd make sure tough guy kept his eyes on the firefighter, too. It was possible she'd stashed it somewhere else.

Nick stretched in satisfaction. The boss had been talking lately about going back home for a spell. It would be nice, he decided. So much simpler there, much slower paced. He'd miss the luxuries, of course, but they'd be back, he knew. The boss wasn't going to relinquish all his interests here.

Maybe he'd have enough to buy the camera before they left. At the very least he'd take his fishing gear. There really wasn't anything better than fishing anyway, no matter where you did it.

Ivy woke at a little after eight the next morning. For a moment, she snuggled deeper in the bed, trying to stave off the memory. It didn't last long. Someone had been in her apartment and searched through every one of her belongings. If Tim hadn't been there... The thought made her skin prickle. The same person was probably out this very minute trying to hunt Moe down. She attempted to wash away the feelings with a hot shower.

Dressed, with a warm cup of coffee in her hands, she felt better. Somehow, some way, she would find Moe and cajole him into telling her what Cyril had given him. He had to, before someone else got killed. She opened the door to search for a newspaper.

Tim stood there, arm raised to knock. He wore the same clothes from the night before, his hair standing up in sections on his head, a shadow of beard on his chin. "Good morning."

"What are you doing here so early?"

He yawned and clasped a hand to his lower back. "I never left. I spent the night in Moe's apartment on his couch. Man, that thing has rocks in the cushions or something."

"You spent the night at Moe's?"

"Yeah. I thought I'd keep an ear out for intruders and maybe Moe, if he came back. Madge gave me the key."

Her heart squeezed. "Oh, Tim. You are so sweet to me, but I can take care of myself. You didn't have to do that."

He grinned. "I know, but think of the advantages. I'm here to give you a ride to church. We're having a special sunrise service today, the one I told you about, to hear some testimonies and such, before everyone heads off to work. Can't pass that up, right? I'll even spring for a donut on the way."

She didn't want to go. As a matter of fact, it had been years since she'd set foot in a church of any kind. She knew, however, that if she didn't, he would be reluctant to leave her alone with a prowler on the loose. "What kind of donut?"

"Whatever you want—sprinkles, jelly-filled, sugar, the works."

She heaved a sigh. "Okay, but just this once."

"Excellent."

Fifteen minutes later Ivy munched on a cinnamon twist as Tim called Madge and asked if he could extend his stay in Moe's apartment for the upcoming week. Madge was only too happy to have someone there in case Moe came home. As Tim drove to church, Ivy picked up a notepad covered with atrocious handwriting. She flipped through page after page of numbers, some crossed out, some circled.

"What is this?"

"Oh, I've just been messing around with that sequence of letters and numbers Moe kept babbling."

"Well what does it mean?"

They pulled up at church. "I'm not sure, but I think I'm onto something. I'll tell you after church."

Ivy bit back her surging curiosity and followed him inside. She was hit by a wave of unpleasant emotion. Sadie's memorial service came back in all its sad detail—the smell of candles, the sound of many mourners filing in, the drone of the pastor's voice.

On that day church had become a place of pain and anger, a home for a God who had punished her beyond measure by taking away her sister. It was ironic that her brother and mother found solace in church, a place to heal from their loss. She couldn't understand it. Her fingers clenched into fists as she sat stiffly next to Tim. He reached for her hand, but she pulled it away.

He'd managed to convince her to come, but it didn't mean she had to like it.

The songs were sweet and soft, followed by the pastor's opening remarks. At one time she would have agreed with his message to obey and seek His word, but it did not reach her now. Then he called a speaker to come forward and give testimony, a tall, balding man named Eugene who had lost his wife to cancer.

Eugene spoke haltingly, often stopping to recover his composure. He talked about how the loss, though expected, was almost more than he could bear. Ivy leaned forward, feeling as if he plucked the thoughts from her own heart.

"I felt like when she died, I did, too. My soul was dry and dead to love after she was gone."

Then he spoke of acceptance, and the myriad people who'd stepped forward to help him through, people sent by a loving God who grieved along with him. "They held me up when I couldn't do it myself. God put their hands here to minister to me."

Ivy stiffened. She stole a glance at Tim, his eyes soft, compassion painted across his handsome face. She wanted to stand up and shout a question at the man. *Why did God let your wife sicken and die? Did you ever wonder why a loving God would allow that?*

Eugene finished after another pause. "I don't know why He took my wife, but I do know that He blessed me very richly by putting her into my life in the first place."

Ivy thought of her sister's face, not as she'd last seen it but as she had many times before—laughing, smiling, her eyes sparkling with fun. A thought jolted through her like an electric current. Roddy's words came back to her. *I choose to remember how she lived, not how she died.*

Had she been so angry, so devastated, that she'd forgotten all of the joy and love she'd shared with Sadie? In her fury, had she stripped the blessing of her sister from her memories? Reduced an amazing lifetime to one horrific last moment?

She looked again at Tim, who gazed back at her and whispered in her ear.

"He loves you, Ivy. God loves you. Can you feel it?"

A flood of coolness made her skin prickle all over. She opened

her mouth to reply, but found she had no words. God loved her?
When she had hated Him so very much for what seemed like a
lifetime? Sadie had always felt God's love and Ivy knew instinctively that if the situation were reversed her sister would not
have turned away from the Lord. Why had she turned her back
on God and all the joy that she'd shared with Sadie? A kaleidoscope of feelings shifted inside her until the notes of the ending
song died away.

Feeling numb and depleted, she followed him back to the truck.

He opened the door for her. "You okay?"

She nodded.

She wanted to ask him about the odd feeling inside her. Was
it peace? Was it relief? Was it the first blush of joy? What had
happened to her heart, sitting on that hard-backed pew amidst a
crowd of strangers? Why couldn't she feel the heavy stone of
anger that she'd carried for years?

She had to think about things, to puzzle her way through the
strange thoughts and feelings that cropped up during that brief
service. It was something she had to do alone, in the quiet of her
own heart. She cleared her throat. "Tell me about your theory,
Tim, the one about Moe's letters and numbers."

"All right," he said as he eased the truck onto the road. "But
you're not going to believe it."

FIFTEEN

Tim fanned through the pages on his notepad, grateful that he'd been able to take the day off. They sat at the coffee shop across the street from the bookstore and sipped as they talked. His excitement grew. "I've been looking at this phrase that Moe's been repeating. His mom said he's always had an affinity for numbers, but there are letters mixed in here, too."

"So what did that tell you?"

"Not a thing, at first. The numbers didn't fall into any particular sequence like a phone number or anything like that."

"And?"

He took a deep breath. "And I remembered my Boy Scout training. We worked on a badge about codes."

She stared at him. "Tim, are you saying this is a code somehow?"

"I think so. Look." He pushed the notepad over to her and wrote Moe's strange phrase on it.

M4e2d7s9c3i6z5t5r472cla0n7noe6r5y9r9o7w2.

"At first I tried circling every second letter or number but that didn't get me anywhere. I assigned a number to each letter of the alphabet, but that was a wash, too."

"You really did pay attention in Boy Scouts."

"You bet I did, and look at this." He eagerly fished a pencil out of his pocket. "If you eliminate every other letter or number, watch what happens."

He made hurried slash marks across the page. Something materialized on the paper.

Medsciztr7canneryrow.

She looked at him. "Well, that's neat, Tim, but it still doesn't mean a whole lot."

"Let's put the spaces in." He rewrote the words.

Medsci. ZTR7. Cannery Row.

"It looks like something, but I still don't get it."

He sat up straighter. "I didn't either until I did more research. You'll never guess what I found out. Medsci happens to be a world-class pharmaceutical company right here in Oregon."

"You're kidding."

"Nope. And guess what new experimental drug they're working on?"

"Does it start with a Z?"

"Uh-huh. ZTR7 to be exact."

She gasped in amazement. "How did Moe get hold of that info? It must have been in whatever Cyril gave him. What does the Cannery Row mean?"

He exhaled, feeling again the frustration about the missing pieces of the puzzle. "That's the part I'm not sure about. There's no place around here called Cannery Row. I know there's one in Monterey, California, but I couldn't find any connection between there and Medsci."

She glanced across the street. "Of course, there's a book by that name, too. Let's go get a copy, just for kicks."

"This is kind of crazy. Should we call Detective Greenly?"

"As you said, this is kind of crazy. Maybe we should work it through a little more first."

"I'm game." He flipped open his laptop. "Why don't you go talk to Mr. Evans at the bookstore? I'm going to do some more research on Medsci."

He watched her walk away, hair blowing in the slight breeze, slender shoulders braced in determination. *Come on, Tim, you can do it.*

Turning to the screen, he willed himself to find the clue that would enable him to keep her safe.

Mr. Evans greeted Ivy with a smile in the bookstore. "Hello, Ms. Beria. How was church?"

"Fine. How did you know I went to church?"

He pointed to her silk blouse. "A customer told me there was a special service this morning and that's not your usual outfit."

She laughed. "I guess not. Mr. Evans, what can you tell me about *Cannery Row?*"

His pale forehead creased. "I assume you mean Steinbeck's *Cannery Row?*"

"Unless there's another one."

He laughed softly. "Not that I'm aware of. Well, let's see. It was published in 1945, I believe. It's basically a story about outsiders struggling to find their place in the world. The characters are unforgettable and poignantly drawn." He hesitated. "I wouldn't think the material would be much to your taste. Are you taking a literature class?"

"No, no. A friend was talking to me about it and I wondered, that's all. Do you have a copy?"

He came out from behind the desk. "What kind of a bookstore would I be if I didn't?" He went to a thick oak shelf and removed a paperback copy. "Here you go. The last one. I guess you're not the only one interested in Steinbeck lately."

She reached for her purse and realized she hadn't brought it. "Oh, man. Can I bring the money by later?"

"I got it," a familiar voice said.

Ivy looked up to see Antonio, tanned and smiling, handing some bills to Mr. Evans.

Her heart thumped. "You don't need to do that."

"No problem. My little contribution to the Ivy fund. Want to get a cup of coffee?"

"Coffee?" She felt disoriented as she thanked Mr. Evans and walked toward the door. "Did you come to the bookstore to ask me to coffee?"

He laughed. "Nah. I was here arranging some training with Chief Strong. I saw you come in when I drove by. Well? How about that coffee?"

"Um, no. I really can't. Tim is waiting for me."

Antonio raised an eyebrow. "Carnelli? The computer geek?"

Ivy felt an irritation stir inside her. "He's not a geek. He's been helping me search for a missing person, a friend of mine."

"Yeah, I heard about that. He won't mind if you come have a cup of coffee." He hesitated. "Or are you two an item?"

She stifled the urge to fire off a sarcastic remark. "We're trying to help a friend, that's all, and we've got work to do today."

Antonio shrugged and they emerged into the bright sunlight. Across the street, Ivy saw Mitch sitting with Tim. "Why don't you join us? The guys would love to talk to you."

He waved at Tim and Mitch. "No, thanks. I've gotta get moving. I'll call you soon."

She watched him go, striding confidently down the street.

Mitch gave her a gentle squeeze when she joined them. "Hi, V. What are you and Tim plotting? He's acting like a secret agent or something."

"Plotting? Nothing much." She wondered why Tim hadn't filled her cousin in. Perhaps he thought the notion was so far-fetched it was laughable.

Mitch eyed the book in her hand. "Doing a little reading?"

"Maybe. I'm thinking I should take up a nice restful hobby until I get my job back."

"You? Restful? That's a good one. How's your recovery looking, anyway?"

"I went to talk to the chief yesterday because I got a message from her, only it wasn't from her. It was some kind of a hoax."

His dark eyes widened. "Really?"

"Yes. To lure me away from my apartment so someone could toss it."

His mouth dropped open. "Toss it? How bad?"

"Let's just say I'm going to be cleaning for the rest of the week."

He slumped in the chair. "Oh, man. That's awful. I'm sorry."

She shrugged. "It's down to a manageable size, thanks to Tim."

"Just call me the Clean Machine." He winked at Ivy. "You ready to go?"

"Uh, sure. Yeah. Let's do that." She gave Mitch a kiss on the cheek. "Are you doing okay?"

He nodded. "Yes, I'm okay and, no, I'm not gambling."

She sighed inwardly. "I knew you weren't."

Tim coughed. "We're going to search for Moe this afternoon. Why don't you come help?"

He gave them a sad glance. "You don't have to babysit me."

"It's not babysitting. We could use another set of eyes."

"Okay." Mitch stood up. "Why don't we go now then? I've got some downtime. I'd be happy to help you beat the bushes."

Tim hesitated. "The police are combing the area this morning, and Ivy and I need to run an errand."

"Where to? Maybe I'll come along."

"Sorry. My truck only seats two comfortably. I'll call you when I get back."

Mitch watched them get into the truck. Ivy waved as they drove off. "Why didn't you tell him about our wacky theory?"

Tim shrugged. "I'm not sure. I guess I figured with all the worries he's got on his plate right now, he didn't need a crazy thing like that to ponder."

Ivy wondered if that was the only reason, but she didn't press.

"I got the book. Mr. Evans was informative as usual, but I don't see how it will help with this Moe business. What errand are you talking about, by the way?"

"First, I thought you might want to change into your play clothes and grab your radio pager and backpack."

"Why, will I need them?"

"You won't, but I know you feel happier when you can hear what kind of action your crew is getting."

She blushed. How did he know her so well? "Where are we going?"

"Medsci's main facility is an hour from here in Maple Grove. The man in charge of the ZTR7 project is a fellow by the name of Roger Smalley. I thought we might pay him a visit."

She shook her head. "You are amazing, Tim. Really amazing."

"Why, thank you. I aim to please."

As they rolled along, she noticed how the sunlight painted his forehead and the strong line of his jaw in a golden profile. *You do please me and I want to please you, too,* she thought with a shock. How had she not noticed it before? Because something had been in the way. Her mind wandered back to the moment in church where, for a second, she had let go of the anger and remembered Sadie.

Sadie would have liked Tim. The thought had never occurred to her before, but she knew it was true. He wasn't the loud, here-I-am kind of hero like Antonio. He was something much better, much quieter, much stronger, and Sadie would have figured that out long before she had, fool that she was. She realized in that moment that she was richly blessed to have them both in her life and her heart.

He looked over. "What are you thinking about over there?"

She felt her cheeks warm. "Nothing. I was just remembering something I'd forgotten."

He looked at her strangely for a minute. "Okay."

Unexpectedly, Antonio surfaced in her thoughts. She thought they were done, but here he was asking her to coffee. She'd once longed for that day. Now she wasn't so sure.

After a quick change of clothes, she joined Tim on the road again. True to Tim's prediction, she had brought the radio along, but kept it turned low. The steady hum of radio traffic soothed her, reminded her of the goal. Find Moe, get her job back. Those were the only two things that mattered, at least that's what she had told herself all along. Now she wondered if there might be another person to add to the equation. And it wasn't just Antonio who filled her mind.

She blinked away her kaleidoscope of feelings and tried to focus on Tim's laptop screen while the miles on the highway crept by. The temperature rose as the sun shone in full glory overhead. It would probably top ninety again. Ivy eased on the air conditioner.

"So what is ZTR7 exactly?"

"A drug to treat autoimmune diseases. It's in the early clinical trial phase but it's showing promise, according to the scant research I've been able to find. The company is playing it close to the vest, letting out enough information to pique the interest of stockholders while holding back to protect their research."

Ivy thought of Cyril and her heart squeezed. "What does this possibly have to do with a guy like Cyril? He didn't seem like the type to be interested in medical research."

"I don't know. Whatever the secret was, it was a big enough reason for someone to kill him."

"We've got to figure this out, for Moe's sake." She thought of the poor guy, alone somewhere, upset by his friend's murder. "Any word from Madge on Moe's whereabouts?"

"No. I called her this morning. She said the police are doing everything they can. Some of her church family has organized a search. She'd be out there pounding the pavement, too, I'm sure, but she doesn't feel well."

They spent the next few miles brainstorming places to look for Moe after their mission at the drug company.

An hour later they pulled into the parking lot of Medsci. The building was several stories high, a modern testament to sleek design.

"Are we just going to walk in and ask to speak to Roger Smalley?"

Tim nodded. "I don't see how else to do it."

"What reason are we going to give for wanting to see him?"

He looked sheepish. "I figured it would come to me eventually."

They headed through the mirrored glass doors of the Medsci lobby. A woman in a chic black suit sat behind a polished wood desk. "May I help you?"

Tim gave her a charming smile. "Hello. Yes, we would like to speak to a Roger Smalley. I understand he's a researcher here?"

Her smile was cool. "We don't disclose that kind of information. May I ask what business you need to discuss?"

Ivy edged closer. "We need to talk to him about a personal matter regarding a mutual friend." She was banking on the fact that Roger knew Cyril or Moe at least in passing.

Her delicate eyebrow arched. "Can you be more specific please?"

"No," they both said in unison.

Tim opened his mouth but she held up a hand. "Why don't you have a seat and I'll make a call. What did you say your names were?"

Tim and Ivy repeated the information and dutifully sat in black padded chairs.

"Do you think we were convincing?" Ivy whispered.

"Convincingly suspicious," he whispered back.

The well-dressed lady hung up. "I'm sorry. There is no one available to speak with you now. Perhaps you can submit a comment or question via our Web site and someone will get back to you."

Ivy gave her a bright smile. "Oh, we're not in a hurry. We don't mind waiting."

She frowned. "Really, I think it wouldn't be a good idea. We don't have any personnel available to speak to you until next week sometime."

"We'll settle for talking to someone about the ZTR7 project." Ivy noticed a door in the corridor above them open. A man with a shiny bald head peered over the balcony, which looked down onto the lobby. He gave them a quick look before retreating to his office and quickly shutting the door.

"I'm sorry," the woman repeated. "It just isn't possible. You are welcome to wait, but there won't be any benefit to it. If you'll excuse me, I have work to do." She turned away from them and began typing on her computer, her face bare of any emotion.

Tim looked out the enormous entrance doors. "That's okay. No problem. Thanks for your help."

He grabbed Ivy's hand and hustled her out the door.

"Where are we going? I thought we would wait a while and see who came out."

"Perfect plan. Why wait?" He pointed to the tall, balding man who was heading in the same direction, his back to them. A leather briefcase with a paper sticking out the bottom was tucked under his arm.

They hustled to catch up with him. "Mr. Smalley?" Tim called.

The man stiffened and continued to move away.

"Mr. Smalley, we know it's you. We have a question to ask."

He rustled in his pocket for the keys to a sleek green Jaguar. As he stumbled over an uneven spot on the pavement, the keys went flying. Ivy snatched them up.

"Here you go, Mr. Smalley." She kept a firm grip on the keys. "Just one question first."

His shoulders sagged, forehead furrowing into wrinkles on his speckled scalp. Ivy noticed that his eyebrows were so fair they almost seemed invisible on his face.

He looked quickly from Tim to Ivy. "You don't look like the police."

Tim frowned. "We're not."

"What do you want?"

"A friend of ours is missing. His name is Moe. He told us about you and ZTR7 before he disappeared," Tim said. "We thought you could help."

Mr. Smalley's eyes narrowed. "I don't know anybody named Moe. How did he know about ZTR7? Most of our research is secret."

Ivy shrugged. "We don't know how he knew. It might be connected to another man named Cyril Donovan. Ever met him?"

"No." A bead of sweat popped out on the man's pale forehead and slid down his nose. Ivy watched it quiver there.

"I don't understand why either of them might have connected my name to ZTR7. I'm only involved peripherally. There are many others more intimately connected than I am. Why me? Why did he use my name?"

Tim held up a calming hand. "We're not sure. That's what we wanted to ask you about."

Mr. Smalley clutched his briefcase even tighter. "Listen. I'm a researcher. I don't know anything. I don't know who sent you, but whoever it is, tell them I'm not involved." With a catlike motion he snatched the keys out of Ivy's hand and jammed them into the car-door lock. In a second the engine roared to life and he left them in a cloud of exhaust.

"What just happened here?" Ivy said as she slid into the passenger seat of Tim's truck.

"I'm not sure."

"He's scared of someone."

"Yes, but he looked sincere when he said he didn't know about a Cyril or a Moe."

"I didn't even get a chance to ask him about Cannery Row. Maybe it's a code name for another project they're working on."

"Could be. Where to now?"

Ivy consulted their scrawled list of places to look for Moe. "How about a trip to Pochono Wilderness Park?"

"Do you really think Moe would go there?"

"His mother said they went together last month, so it's a place he knows."

Tim sighed. "This is like looking for the proverbial needle."

"Let's just pray we find the right haystack soon."

SIXTEEN

Ivy called Madge while Tim ordered sandwiches. She was clicking off the phone when she saw Mitch across the street, deep in conversation with Charlie. Charlie pulled his cowboy hat lower over his eyes and handed Mitch a folded piece of paper. He looked up and saw Ivy, then ducked his head and continued on as Mitch crossed the street to join her.

Through narrowed eyes, she watched Charlie start up his Porsche and drive away.

"Hi, Mitch. How's Charlie doing?"

"Fine."

"What did he give you?"

Mitch's lip crimped. "It's just a work schedule. Nothing shady. I'm covering some extra shifts for a buddy of mine."

She wanted to pry more, but Tim returned with sandwiches. "Oh, hi, Mitch. Reporting for search duty? Want half a sandwich?"

"No, thanks. Have you heard from Moe?"

Ivy shook her head. "No. We're just as in the dark as the rest of the searchers."

"Really? I would have thought he'd have called you."

"Not a word."

"That's really weird. Not even a note or anything?"

She was surprised at the suspicion on his face. "No. No note. Why would I keep a thing like that to myself when there's a whole team of people looking for him?"

He shrugged. "Dunno. Where are we headed first?"

Ivy filled him in while they munched. She pulled out a picture Madge had given her of Moe and let Mitch have a look before they drove to the park. Mitch followed in Ivy's car.

On the way her PDA beeped. She fished it out and checked the screen. "Is it Thursday?"

"Uh-huh."

"Yes," she chortled, reaching for the straps on her sling. "I get to take this thing off for a few hours."

"I assume the doctor told you to take it easy?"

"Yes, she did. I have to put it back on if there's pain, but don't you see? I'm one step away from starting therapy and that means…"

"Two steps away from getting your job back?"

She laughed. "You bet."

"That's great, Ivy."

She thought she heard a shade of regret in his tone. "What's wrong?"

"Nothing, nothing. I'm happy you'll get your job back soon. I know how much you love it."

"But…?"

"I'll just miss you, is all."

"Why? I won't be going anywhere."

"Not physically. Let's face it, when you're back in firefighting mode, I'm the odd man out."

She was surprised. "Do I make you feel like that?"

"Not intentionally, I'm sure. I guess when you have such a strong brotherhood that means so much to you, there isn't much room left over for civilians."

She put a hand on his arm. "Hey, I'm sorry, Tim. I didn't mean to do that." She knew with a guilty certainty she'd fostered an arrogance that blinded her to people outside her beloved profession. Outsiders couldn't relate, wouldn't understand. The thought pained her. She resolved to make it up to him.

He gave her a grin. "It's okay. It's been great not having to share you with all those hero types for a while."

For some unaccountable reason, a verse from long ago surfaced in Ivy's mind.

He leads the humble in justice and He teaches the humble His way. Psalm 25:9.

She could not explain why it had popped into her head but the words reminded her of Tim. He was so good and so humble, words she could not use to describe herself, but she knew that God must love her anyway to put him into her life. She felt again the strange peace that had washed over her at church.

She patted his shoulder, feeling suddenly like a scared child, at the mercy of feelings she'd avoided for so long. "I'll…I'll make time, even when I get my job back. Maybe, sometimes, we can, you know, go to church together or something."

He looked at her, eyes round with amazement. "Ivy, there is nothing I would like better than that. I'm so glad you've changed your mind."

"Don't get me wrong, I've still got plenty of anger, Tim. I don't understand or accept things the way you do, but maybe I can try."

He squeezed her hand. "I'll be right there for you, every step, I promise."

Her heart was too filled for her lips to answer. She squeezed back, wanting to tell him how important he was, but she knew it was not fair to bolster his hopes until she'd sorted out her own mess of feelings.

The warmth of his fingers on her skin reminded her he was interested in more than friendship. He was right when he said she belonged to a brotherhood, a brotherhood that was still her whole life. But could she make room for him? Could she really open herself up to that kind of vulnerability again? The thought scared her and she gently withdrew her hand from his.

He cleared his throat. "So what's our plan of attack here?"

"Cover as much ground as possible. Madge thought he would have stayed near the visitor center and the spot where they picnicked. He is afraid of climbing, fortunately, so that eliminates a lot of area. This is really the only park he could have gotten to on foot around here."

They turned onto the gravel road that led to the park entrance. Ivy marveled again at the distant mountains, framed against a brilliant blue sky. In their severe perfection, they looked like some fantastic oil painting. Mitch pulled into the parking place next to them. Ivy handed him a backpack and clipped the radio to her belt.

He groaned as he shouldered the load. "What do you have in here? Bowling balls?"

"Funny. Some supplies, is all. You should know how quickly things can change in the wilderness, even within miles of town."

Tim pulled some bottles of water from a cooler. "Keeps the rescue people in business."

"Yeah. We've transported plenty of weekend-warrior types who had a sudden yen for the great outdoors." She read over the notes Moe's mother had given her. "Madge said they visited the nature center and stopped for a picnic along Thimbleberry Creek."

Tim headed the group toward the visitor center. He showed Moe's picture to a docent and park ranger. Neither had seen the man. Venturing back out into the heat, they walked through fields of wild onion and yarrow, down to the meandering creek.

They stopped to rest in the shade of some massive huckleberry bushes. Overhead in the trees, a woodpecker poked forlornly for bugs. A sharp-shinned hawk floated in lazy circles in the intensely blue sky. Ivy looked at the creek, greatly depleted by the summer heat.

Mitch tossed a pebble into the water. "Well, if he's camping out here, I hope he knows enough not to drink the water."

The crystal-clear water housed plenty of parasitic *Giardia,* Ivy knew. Would Moe be able to survive much longer without such basic knowledge? He only knew how to cook microwave popcorn. His mother prepared the rest of his dinners and stocked his fridge. Her stomach spasmed with worry. "If we don't find him soon, giardiasis will be the least of his troubles."

They combed every inch of the creek until it tumbled downstream into a steep rocky crevice. "You don't suppose he..." Tim started.

"No, I'm sure he didn't. Madge said Moe is afraid to hike or climb. He wouldn't attempt to head down there." In spite of her confident pronouncement, she trained the binoculars over the rocks and down along the surface of the lake, finding no sign of Moe. With a sigh of relief, she wiped her sweating brow, and they headed back to the car.

Mitch finished a bottle of water. "Where to next?"

Ivy eyed him in surprise. "You're really sticking with this rescue effort, Mitch. I'm impressed."

"Hey, I can be altruistic when the need arises." He slam-dunked the bottle into a recycling container. "Are you sure he didn't leave you a message? Some sort of papers that could be a clue?"

"I'm sure."

"Did you look through his apartment?"

"We did and so did the police. Tim's been staying there and he hasn't found anything either."

Mitch shot him a look. "Could be he doesn't know what he's looking for."

"Could be," Tim agreed. "Do you have any ideas what kind of clue we might be overlooking?"

Mitch shrugged. "Nah, how could I? I've never met the kid."

Ivy flipped pages in her notebook as they returned to the parking lot. "The only other place that County Search and Rescue isn't covering is the outdoor strip mall at the edge of town. Madge visited there with Moe a few months back. She said they bought some of Homer's fudge and looked at the fish in the aquarium store."

Tim opened the door for her. "Why do I feel the need for some fudge right now?"

She laughed as she jumped in, grateful again to have Tim to interject some lightness into the search.

When they were back on the road, she meant to turn the radio pager down to barely audible but hit the squelch button instead. They both jumped as the loud static crackle filled the space. "Sorry." Ivy readjusted. "My shoulder isn't quite up to snuff."

"Is it aching?"

"A little." She read the expression on his face. "I'll put the sling back on after our next stop. See? I can do the prudent thing when necessary."

"I have no doubt about it."

"What did Detective Greenly say when you told him about Roger Smalley?"

Tim sighed. "There was a long moment of silence, which I interpreted to mean 'why are you poking around in police business?' Then he seemed pretty interested. They're strained to the limit, between Cyril's murder, the search and rescue for Moe and general police business. He said he was going to try to recruit some help and look into the Smalley connection."

Ivy waved to three women she recognized as they drove by several ranches and a chicken farm. They were knocking on doors, showing Moe's picture, she was sure. It made her feel a bit better to know they were only a small part of the rescue effort. *God...* The thought popped into her head before she could stop it. But how to ask? How to talk to Him when it had been such a very long time? She felt Tim's eyes on her. "I was just, I don't know, thinking about a prayer or something..."

He took her hand. "Lord, help us to find Moe. Keep him safe and give him peace, knowing that You love him. Amen."

Ivy's smile was sheepish. "I think I'm not good at that kind of thing anymore."

"Just tell Him what's on your mind."

Her heart skipped a beat at the tenderness in his eyes. For a moment she despaired of ever figuring out the tangle of emotion that swept through her.

Tim pulled up to the strip of wood-fronted stores. A scant handful of tourists strolled the sidewalks, sipping sodas and clutching plastic shopping bags. The smell of chocolate filled the air as they got out of the truck.

Mitch joined them.

The rail-thin woman at the fudge shop remembered seeing Moe and his mother. "Oh, yeah. He was a funny one, wouldn't look at me. Only ate a mouthful of fudge, but he seemed to really enjoy it. His mother did most of the talking for him."

"Have you seen him recently? He's missing." Ivy showed him the picture to refresh her memory.

Her face crinkled in sympathy. "Missing? What a trial for his mother. No, I'm sorry. I haven't seen him, but then sometimes I don't even see the light of day when I'm working, 'specially when a tour group comes through or something. I'll be sure to call the police if I do see him around."

She insisted they each take a piece of fudge to "keep their strength up for the search." Ivy didn't feel very strong as they headed out into the blistering heat. She knew the longer a person stayed missing, especially a person at risk, the worse the outcome would probably be. Moe must be terrified, wherever he was.

She forced her feet to start moving to the next stop: the bicycle shop across the street. The young kid working on a ten-speed tugged on his earring thoughtfully. "Oh, yeah. I remember him."

Ivy's heart sped up. "He was here? When?"

The kid took off his baseball hat and wiped the sweat from his forehead. "Yesterday, looking at the bikes."

Tim's eyes widened. "Did he talk to you? Did he say anything at all?"

"Uh-huh. Never came into the shop, just sort of hung around. When I tried to talk to him he looked all freaked and ran away." The boy's eyes narrowed. "He came back, though, when I was on my break. I lost two weeks' pay because of him."

Ivy frowned. "What do you mean?"

The clerk pointed to a spot at the end of a line of motor scooters. "We rent those out, man, and now there's one missing since your boy showed up. He boosted one of our bikes."

Ivy could not suppress a groan. She knew it wasn't in Moe's character to steal, but he was clearly desperate. Now the search circle had to be widened to accommodate a vehicle. Moe could be anywhere.

Mitch, Ivy and Tim exchanged a look of despair. They thanked the boy and returned to the truck to call Detective Greenly.

Mitch made a phone call as well before he retrieved another bottle of water. "Where are we going to look now?"

"I'm not sure." Ivy sank onto the front bumper. "I'm open to suggestions."

"I just talked to Charlie and filled him in. He's going to see about taking his personal chopper up and check things out. I said I'd go over and help him."

Ivy felt a surge of guilt, remembering how she'd accused Charlie the last time they'd met and for her rampant suspicion of the man. "Wow. That is really kind of him. Would you tell him I said thank you? I'll tell him myself when I can."

"Sure. So where are you two headed while we're up in the air?"

Ivy looked at Tim.

He shrugged. "Well, I still think he'd stay off the main highway so let's go north toward Two Pines for a while. What do you say?"

"I say it's better than any idea I can come up with." Ivy hugged Mitch and they parted company.

She was buckling her seat belt when the dispatcher's calm voice on her radio pager cut through the air.

Caller reports victim is a young male, Caucasian.

The last words hit the hardest.

Unresponsive at the bottom of the ravine.

SEVENTEEN

Ivy's heart was in her throat. They drove as fast as the law would allow to Rock City, a small area of a much larger wilderness park that featured rugged boulders heaped in a pile. The formation seemed to attract amateur climbers the way flowers beckoned hummingbirds. Many a time her crew had responded to various falls and rescues of people who didn't realize climbing boulders without any training or equipment could be dangerous. Or fatal.

The memory flooded in before she could stop it.

Teen male, cut school to climb with his buddies. Fell twenty feet.

They bagged him, pulled on gloves to protect against blood that covered seemingly every inch of him.

Preassessment.

Eyes wide, pupils dilated. Skin ashen.

No pulse or respiration.

Put on the C-collar.

Five compressions, two ventilations, five and two, five and two.

Shock on the faces of his friends.

Keep trying while they hook up defibrillator.

Keep trying.

Haul him up and load him in the ambulance.

Run the tape to check for life.

The captain's voice, strong but sad. "We've got a straight line. Let's call it."

Straight line.
No life left.
No hope left.

With great effort, she shook off the memory, realizing that she had Tim's hand in a death grip as they drove.

"You okay?"

She managed a nod.

By the time they arrived, the firefighters were hauling up the victim, strapped to a board, using a winch powered by the engine. She noted with displeasure that Denise was waiting, paramedic box at the ready, to treat the victim.

Adrienne Strong talked on her radio, then waved to Ivy and Tim. "What brings you by?"

Ivy cleared her throat. "Um, we thought the victim might be the man we're looking for."

One eyebrow lifted in surprise. "The kid? I didn't think you knew him. You're helping with the search?"

I've got to do something to keep busy while I'm barred from work, she thought. *Control yourself, Ivy. Keep your sour grapes where they belong.* "Yes, he's a friend of ours and a neighbor, too."

She nodded. "Okay. We're bringing him up now."

The guys guided the backboard up and over the edge of the ravine.

Ivy's breath froze.

How could she tell Madge? After all the woman had been through. How could she tell her Moe was dead?

When Ivy saw the bundled victim's head, she sagged against Tim in relief. Red hair, shocking curly red hair, poked out from the man's head as it was secured to the backboard. A redhead, it was not Moe.

Denise set to work on the victim immediately, and Ivy grudgingly had to admit the woman was competent. Ivy was further relieved to hear that the man had a pulse. It comforted her to know that someone else's mother would not receive devastating news.

Her own mother's face surfaced in her mind. She thought for a moment what she must have felt when she got the news about

Sadie. She had to have been broken, crushed by grief, yet she had never once let go of her faith.

Tim reached an arm around her shoulders. "What are you thinking?"

"I was thinking that my mother is a strong woman, much stronger than I could ever be."

"Mothers are like that."

She thought, too, about how her own rejection of God for many long years must have further saddened her mother. Her breath caught. "I could have been a much better daughter."

He brushed a kiss across her temple. "Your mother wouldn't trade you in for anything, and neither would I."

She snuggled into his strong chest for a moment, allowing herself to be comforted. Then the firefighters began to clamber up over the edge of the ravine. "Let's go."

"Don't you want to say hi to your guys?"

She shook her head. "They've got work to do, and so do we."

"The search is still on?"

She nodded. "You better believe it."

She followed him to the truck without a word.

Tim phoned Madge to check on her and listened intently for a few minutes before hanging up. "She's got a houseful coordinating the next phase of the search. My mom and dad are there."

"I didn't know your folks knew Moe."

"They don't, but Madge attends our church sometimes so they've mobilized to help a fellow member of the flock."

She laughed. "Your parents are great."

He was ridiculously pleased that Ivy got along so well with his folks. "Yes, they are. My mother is probably creating a flowchart to track the whole business, and Dad is more than likely whipping up his spaghetti to keep everyone fully carb loaded. Should we go over and pool our info before we continue the search?"

"Absolutely."

It wasn't spaghetti but lasagna that Mr. Carnelli was pulling hot from the oven when they arrived. He greeted Ivy with a tight hug, squashing her against his chest hard enough to make her wince. His cheeks were shiny from the oven's heat, eyes black and sparkling under a mop of unruly hair.

Tim hugged his dad and grabbed a pot holder to help with the food before he and Ivy wandered into command central.

Mrs. Carnelli stood at the table, her slender form bent over maps and pages of computer printouts. She gave Ivy and Tim a peck on the cheek and pointed to the map. "The areas in red are places we've covered at least once." She sighed. "It was a real wake-up call when you told us Moe probably had access to a motorbike."

Tim looked over the search grids. "We've got a plenty big area left to cover."

She nodded, her freckles vivid against her pale skin. "Yes." She lowered her voice to a whisper. "I'm not sure how much longer the county is going to be able to keep up a full-scale search."

Tim feared the agency was stretched plenty thin. "Has anyone reported finding a trace of him?"

She shook her head. "No. It's as if he evaporated into thin air."

They broke off the conversation as Madge joined them. Tim thought she looked a decade older than she had a few days earlier. Without a word she embraced them with trembling arms. Tim hugged her back and led her to a chair.

"How are you holding up?"

"I don't know. I feel numb. That's better than what I feel when I think of him out there, alone." Her eyes welled up with tears.

Ivy squeezed her shoulder. "We'll find him."

Her head sagged forward against her chest. "Every minute, I expect the phone to ring, to hear his voice." Suddenly her eyes flew open. "Wait a second. I remembered what I wanted to tell you. A man called here the day Moe disappeared. He asked me about some package."

Tim leaned forward, riveted. "What man? What did he say exactly?"

Madge screwed up her face in thought. "He said he was a friend of Cyril's and Cyril was taking care of some papers for him. He saw Cyril around town with Moe and wondered if he had given Moe the papers to look after."

"What did you say?"

"I told him Moe didn't have any papers. When I tried to ask the man what his name was, he hung up."

Tim's skin prickled. "Was his voice distinctive? Did he have an accent or anything?"

"Not that I can remember. Do you think he knows something about my Moe?" Her face drained of color. "Do you think he...did something to Moe?"

Tim hastened to reassure her. "I'm sure he didn't, but I think you'd better call Detective Greenly and tell him what you just told me."

When Madge hung up with the police, her face had an even more ghastly pallor. Mrs. Carnelli insisted that she go lie down.

Tim, Ivy and the Carnellis sat at the table, picking at plates of lasagna. Even the robust Mr. Carnelli seemed to have lost his appetite. Tim put his fork down with a clank. "I can't shake the feeling that this is connected to Medsci somehow. I've searched the Internet as thoroughly as I know how and I can't figure it out. How would Moe get information about an experimental drug?"

His mother cocked her head. "From Cyril, but the question is, how did he get it and why is it significant? Seems to me Roger Smalley's name and connection to the drug are fairly public information. Not worth killing anyone."

"That's my take, too, but Smalley is involved in something, Mom."

Ivy nodded. "He wanted to be anywhere but talking to us, that's for sure."

Mr. Carnelli frowned. "Maybe the drug is something other companies would love to get their hands on."

Tim sighed. "That occurred to me also, but there was no crucial information about the chemical formulas in Moe's message, nothing that would help another company duplicate the compound. I can't figure out the connection."

Ivy could not suppress a yawn as the room slipped into predusk shadows.

Mrs. Carnelli smiled. "Look at you two, completely exhausted. You should go home right now and get some rest."

Ivy shook her head. "We were going to cover more ground today."

She pressed her lips together. "It's getting dark. You won't be any good to anybody if you wear yourselves out completely."

Tim smiled at his mother. Seeing the weariness on Ivy's face, he knew it was sound advice. "That's her 'I mean business' voice. We'll start the search again tomorrow."

Ivy let Mr. Carnelli ply her with a foil-wrapped plate of lasagna and Tim did the same.

"Better take it, Ivy," Tim whispered, "or Dad will sneak it into your bag when you're not looking."

Mr. Carnelli gave him a fake punch. "You should be so lucky to find my lasagna in your bag."

"True." Tim waved goodbye and drove them home, eyeing Ivy as he drove.

"What time do you want to kick things off tomorrow?" she asked around a yawn.

His heart dropped. "I'm sorry to say, I've got to work. I took a few days off, but there's no one to cover for me on Fridays. Can you survive until I get off work at five?" More important, could she stay safe and out of trouble?

She grinned. "It won't be easy, but I'll do my best."

He walked her to her door and waited until she was safely inside. "Good night, Ivy." The sight of her there, framed against the soft apartment light, head tilted slightly, was so very beautiful. He wanted to extend the evening for just a little longer, to let his true feelings out of the cage he'd tried to confine them to. He opened his mouth and then closed it again.

"What were you going to say?"

His face warmed. "Oh, never mind. It's nothing you'd want to hear, I think."

"Go on, tell me."

He looked down at his shoe. "I was going to say that even though we didn't find Moe, I sure am glad I got to spend the day with you."

"Glad? To go tramping through wilderness parks in the blazing heat?"

His eyes locked on hers. "Yes." *Don't you know that when I'm with you, everything is better? No matter where we are or what we're doing. My life is better with you in it.*

Even though his brain told him not to, he couldn't restrain the urge that coursed through him like a fast-moving stream. He kissed her, a long slow kiss that she returned in kind. When he pulled away, they were both speechless.

"Tim, I…"

"I know," he said, turning down the hallway, ignoring the pounding in his chest. "I told you it wasn't what you'd want to hear."

EIGHTEEN

The smoke shrouded Moe in a blanket of darkness. She held her gloved hand out to him, but the sling prevented her from reaching his fingers. His eyes rounded in horror as the smoke closed in on him. He began to rock back and forth, lips wide in a silent scream.

"No, Moe. Come to me. Let me help you," Ivy shouted.

The blackness increased, enveloping all but Moe's terrified face.

Again, she reached out, straining against the bandages that imprisoned her. She watched, helpless, as the smoke funneled into his mouth, choking off his scream.

With a jerk, Ivy shot upright in bed, sweat rolling off her forehead. Her breath came in ragged pants. She sucked in air, trying to steady herself. "Just a dream. Just a dream." Though the nightmare faded away, the urgency it left behind didn't. She had to find Moe. She had to save him.

She didn't take time to eat breakfast before she pulled on clothes and headed out into the warm August morning. After she stopped at Mitch's to pick up her car, she sped out of town. A thick blanket of clouds covered the sky, promising a much-needed summer rain.

In spite of the approaching storm, the campground she'd been assigned to search by Mrs. Carnelli was full to overflowing with kids and parents enjoying the last few weeks of summer vacation. She showed Moe's picture to every camp employee she could find, as well as many guests, with no luck. Stomach hollow with hunger, she finally headed back to the car.

Pieces of glass littered the ground around the driver-side window. Ivy gasped and glanced wildly around, looking for anyone suspicious. There was no one.

Avoiding the glass, she gingerly eased the door open and checked the interior. The contents of the glove box were spilled onto the floor. The upholstery was pulled up from the bucket seats as if someone had been looking for something underneath.

She looked more closely and found the trunk had been popped open, her first-aid kit rifled through, as well.

Desperation swelled inside her. "What do you want from me?" she screamed to no one.

A chilling thought struck her. Maybe whoever had done it was watching her right now, hidden behind the leafy screen of trees. She started to tremble.

"Keep calm, Ivy." She wrapped a jacket around her hand and brushed the glass from the front seat before she jumped inside and revved the engine. She knew she shouldn't move the vehicle until after the police had examined it, but the fear inside filled her with a desperate need to escape.

Only after she was on the road back home did she begin to breathe more easily. She made it back to town and left a message for the detective. Unwilling to go home to her empty apartment, Ivy parked along Main Street and sat on a shaded bench to sip a bottle of water.

Mitch appeared, slouching onto the bench next to her. "Any luck?"

"No, and my car got broken into."

He gasped and went over to take a look at the shattered window. "What is up with that?" he said. "Maybe some punk kids?"

"I don't know." Ivy felt too tired to think about it anymore. "Did you have any luck searching?"

He shook his head. "Charlie and I stayed up for a few hours yesterday. I thought I'd join you on foot today. Where's Tim?"

"Working. Isn't that where you're supposed to be?"

"I took the morning off to help with the search. I have to be back this afternoon."

"That was nice of you."

His gaze wandered down the street.

"Are you meeting someone?"

"Me? No, no." He turned his attention back to her. "So did you give any more thought to those clues? Did you remember anything Moe gave you or anything you saw him carrying around?"

"No, Mitch. I told you that before."

"I know. I'm being thorough, is all."

Ivy's cell phone let out a reminder beep. She checked the display and gasped. "Oh, man. I completely forgot my doctor's appointment. I'm supposed to have the shoulder looked at. I've gotta go. See you later."

Figuring it would be safe to walk down a public street in broad daylight, she hurried the six blocks as quickly as she could, slipping the sling on to impress the doctor. Hope swelled inside with each step. She had been able to use her shoulder and go without the sling for the better part of a day. Things were improving all the time.

Soon it would be back to work.

An image of Tim rose in her mind. Would he feel abandoned again? The thought made her sad. She shook it away. Her work was the most important thing in her life. Wasn't it? She wouldn't lose focus for anyone. Not even Tim.

She scurried up the steps to the clinic past a man sitting in a chair on the cement patio, reading a magazine held tightly against the quickening wind. His blond crew-cut hair was almost the same shade as his pale skin. Something about him seemed familiar.

Her phone rang before she made it inside. "Hey, Mom. I'm going into the doctor's office. No, no luck yet with the search. Look, can I come by and fill you in later? I've got to go now."

As she tried to pocket the phone, a sudden pain in her shoulder made her lose her grip. The cell skittered across the cement, near the man with the magazine. He fished it out from between his feet and handed it to her.

"Thanks so much." She took the phone and he tucked the issue under his arm and rose to hold the door.

Face flushed, she hurried by, glancing at the magazine folded to reveal an article on digital cameras. Inside the office she composed herself and waited for the nurse to lead her to a room.

The doctor did a thorough examination of the burns. "I'm happy with your progress, Ivy. It's definitely healing. I think we'll get out of this with minimal scarring, too."

"Great. How much longer before I can go back on the line?"

His eyebrow lifted. "I was about to say, this is the dangerous time. Your shoulder is feeling better and you've got some mobility back so your tendency will be to overdo it. You've seen the physical therapist, I assume?"

"Yes. She's going to check me out again in a month. But I think I'll be ready before then. You said the burns are healing up nicely, right?"

"Right. So that means when the therapist clears you for rehab, you can start on that shoulder."

"I was hoping, maybe, you could speed things along."

His round face wore an exasperated look. "Give it time, Ivy. The body's power to heal is miraculous, but you've got to let it do the work." He patted her arm and said goodbye.

Ivy left the clinic. Her rumbling stomach demanded attention so she stopped at the bakery for a snack. She was about to find a spot on the bench to enjoy the soft peanut-butter cookie when she noticed the same crew-cut blond-haired man sipping tea. She half smiled at him. He looked up from his magazine, his gray eyes luminous in his pale face. He did not smile, and there was a look to him, an intangible something that made her gut turn to ice.

The chill grabbed hold of her spine. The magazine was still turned to the very same page it had been an hour ago. Though he looked away, she could feel his eyes burning into her as she left. Was it him? Was he the one who tried to take her purse, broke into her house and smashed her car window?

With fear circling her gut, she checked over her shoulder. The man was standing now, discarding his drink and turning in her direction. She dropped the cookie into a trash can and walked as fast as possible away from him, trying to decide how to escape, when a familiar car pulled up at the curb.

Charlie reached over and opened the door to his sports car. "Need a lift?"

She hesitated only a moment before she jumped in and pulled the door closed.

"Where you headed?"

"I was going to visit my mother. She's off Main Street."

"All right, then. Looks like a good storm coming in." He pulled the car smoothly away from the curb, turning on the wipers to catch the first drops of rain. Ivy looked in the sideview mirror at the man with the magazine, who stared at the vehicle as it drove away.

"You okay, Ivy? You look a shade pale."

She tried to control her breathing. Was her imagination making her see villains everywhere? In the safety of Charlie's car, her fears seemed less logical. The guy was probably completely harmless. It had to be a mistake. "I'm fine. Thanks for the ride. What brings you to town?"

"Errands, mostly."

He looked straight ahead and Ivy could make out lines in his face that she hadn't noticed before. He seemed old all of a sudden. "Charlie, I think I owe you an apology."

He started. "You do?"

She swallowed hard. "Yes. It was indiscreet of me to bring Mitch's problem up to a colleague and just plain rude to blame you. I'm sorry."

He sighed, a long gusty sound. "I appreciate the sentiment, Ivy, but I've been doin' some serious thinking about it and I believe it's the other way around."

"What do you mean?"

He drummed his fingers on the steering wheel. "I did introduce Mitch to online gambling. I thought it was fun, a thrill ride. I guess I'm an adrenaline junkie. That's what my two ex-wives will tell you, anyway."

"You didn't make Mitch bet away his savings."

"No, but I sure didn't discourage him from playing. I never thought about the bad side of it. It's all so neat and tidy online, so…impersonal."

"Have you lost much money that way?"

"Yes, ma'am, but not enough that it impacted my life. I got bored of it after a while, turned my attention to other things."

Ivy shook her head. "I sure wish Mitch could have done the same."

"Me, too." Charlie's brow furrowed. "I didn't realize how deep he'd gotten himself in until you came to my house. Now that I think on it, he's been squirrelly for a while, skipping out on trainings, missing social functions, and I remember seeing some guy, a really big guy, talking to him after a shift one day. Mitch didn't look too happy about it."

"Did the man have dark, curly hair?"

"Yeah."

"He's with the mob in New York. He was sent to collect on the money Mitch borrowed from his boss."

Charlie's head sagged against the leather seat. "Oh, man. He's really in deep. If he'd have come to me, I could have made him a loan, no strings attached."

"But you didn't? You're really not the one who bailed him out?"

"No, ma'am. He never asked me." He stopped for the light. "I feel really low about it."

Ivy touched his arm. "You had no idea he would become addicted to gambling. I think things are improving. Tim confiscated his computer and Mitch has promised me up and down that he hasn't placed a bet since."

Charlie grimaced. "Ivy, not to be the bearer of bad news, but I am familiar with addiction. My daddy was an alcoholic and he could charm a snake out of his stripes with his promises to give up liquor. I think he really meant it, too, but some things gotta be kicked with help."

She watched a group of kids running in a front yard as they drove along. "So you think he's still gambling?"

"I don't know." Charlie frowned. "He's getting weird phone calls that seem to upset him."

Though she hated to admit it, Mitch's behavior had seemed odd to her lately, too.

Charlie turned onto her mother's street and she pointed out the house. On impulse she said, "Have you seen a blond guy with a crew cut hanging around Mitch?"

"Can't say as I have. You figure New York has sent someone else to keep tabs on him?"

Ivy got out of the car and leaned into the open window. "I'm not sure. See if you can spot anyone unusual today when Mitch reports in this afternoon."

Charlie frowned. "Did he tell you he's on duty later?"

She nodded.

"Now I'm really worried."

"Why?"

Charlie stared at her. "Our schedule shifted, Ivy. Mitch doesn't work today."

NINETEEN

Ivy's mouth began to water as soon as she crossed the threshold of her mother's house. The smell of roasted garlic and simmering beans tickled her nose. She found Juana in the backyard under an umbrella, picking fat red tomatoes.

"Hi, Mama. Is that great smell in the kitchen what I think it is?"

"Of course," she said with a smile. "Red beans and rice, and don't tell me you're not hungry. I can hear your stomach growling from here."

"I'm always hungry for your beans and rice." Ivy picked some of the succulent fruit and helped carry them inside. She pulled up a chair at the table while her mother dished up a bowl of the steaming rice.

"How is the search for Moe going?"

Ivy related, in frustrating detail, their lack of progress. "Madge is so devastated at the thought of losing her son. It made me, well, sort of put in my head…"

"What, Ivy?"

"I guess I never thought about how hard it must have been for you to get past Sadie's death."

She put down her spoon. "Has she been on your mind lately?"

Ivy picked at a grain of rice on the table that had escaped the bowl. "Yes. I, um, Tim took me to church and it sort of started me thinking."

Juana patted Ivy's hand. "Go on, honey. Talk to me."

"There's not much more to tell." Ivy stood up and walked around the room, touching the pictures. "Everything is all jumbled up in my mind lately."

Juana sat in silence, watching her.

"Mama, you said you hear from kids who read your Penny Pocket stories."

"Sometimes. They write letters and draw pictures for me once in a while."

"Do they, have any of them lost people in their lives?"

"A few."

"What do you tell them, when they ask you for advice?"

Her brown eyes were warm. "I don't give advice, honey. I just tell them I know how much it hurts and so does God."

Ivy turned to face her. "How come you didn't get mad? The way she died, it was…" She shuddered.

"It was horrible and I did get mad, beyond mad as a matter of fact. I was enraged at the man who was talking on his car phone instead of paying attention to his driving. I was furious with him for taking my daughter away. I wanted him to be punished. Truth be told, I wanted him to be dead, until I met him face-to-face."

"Then what happened?"

"I found out he was in worse agony than I was because he killed a girl and he didn't have God to ask for forgiveness. He was trapped in a nightmare with no hope of release. Truly, a living hell."

"And that took away your anger?"

"Some." She massaged a kink in her neck. "I went through plenty of rage and depression, Ivy, but I had two other kids and a husband to live for. God entrusted me to be there for all of you and gave me the strength to carry on."

The words bubbled up from the bottom of her soul. "Why did He let it happen? Why did He let her die?"

Juana's eyes were moist. "I don't know, honey. I just don't know. I'll ask Him someday, but He did teach me through Sadie that every moment, every day is a blessed gift and that's how I try to live my life."

Ivy sank down into the chair again. "You're so strong. I wish I could feel that way."

"You could, if you let go of the idea that you're supposed to save every earthly victim you run across."

She bristled. "I was born to be a firefighter."

"No, honey. You were born to be Ivy Beria, child of God. If that means you're a firefighter, great, as long as you don't hide behind that uniform."

"Hide? From what?"

"From people, from loss." Juana took her hands. "From love."

Ivy held her mother's strong fingers, feeling a tide of love connecting them both. She tried to speak, but couldn't.

Juana held on. "Listen to me, sweetheart. Sometimes people stay here for a long time and sometimes they are here for only a brief season. Like Jesus, honey, God's own son. He was here for only a short time, but what He left behind will never be lost."

Ivy felt her eyes fill. "Oh, Mama. I feel so confused. I've been angry at God for so long, hating Him for taking Sadie. Now I'm starting to see that He put so many people in my life to help me along, to help me through and to…"

"Love you?"

Ivy flushed. "I thought I loved Antonio, but I think it was for the wrong reasons." Tim's face swam up in her mind. She saw the sincerity in his eyes, the sweet, kind nature that shone through his soul. Something tickled her stomach, a little sensation that traveled upward into her heart. *Tell him you love him. Admit it, to him and to yourself.* Could she? Should she?

And then what? She knew how attachment ended and it would kill her to lose him. Antonio was one thing, a painful memory, but Tim? He was altogether another. She shook her head.

"I don't know. My mind is all mixed up. I thought I understood everything, but nothing is the same since I lost my job."

"Then maybe it's a good thing you did."

Her head jerked around. "No, no, it's not. Don't get any ideas, Mama. I'm going to get my job back and things will be normal again."

Her mother laughed, a big, warm sound that filled the room. "Oh, honey, nothing is ever normal for very long." She got up and wrapped Ivy in a firm hug.

She let her mother's embrace continue for a minute before she pulled away. "I've got to get back to the search, Mama."

"It's going to pour any minute. Why don't you stay here and help me put up some tomatoes?"

"Don't you have a pantry full already?"

"Sure, but it's not possible to can too much, in my opinion."

Her mother's words set off a lightning strike in her mind. "Maybe that's what he meant."

"Who?"

"Oh, nothing. I've got to go check something out." She kissed her mother. "I'll come visit again soon." She accepted a foil packet of beans and rice before she headed out the door.

On the porch she looked around for any sign of the man with the magazine. She pulled out her cell and dialed Tim's number. He didn't answer so she left a message telling him about her plans. She thought briefly about calling Mitch to come and escort her, but rejected the idea. He was already hovering like a shadow and lying to her about something. It was better not to involve him any further. Pulling her jacket hood on, she started off into the misty afternoon.

The idea was half-crazy and she knew it. Cyril met Moe when he worked at the recycle shack situated on a corner of the local shopping complex. Could Moe's strange message about Medsci and Cannery Row possibly refer to the line of wire bins set up to receive cans? It was a ridiculous notion, but she could not get it out of her mind.

"Oh, brother. Tim will get a good laugh out of this," she muttered as she hustled along. In spite of the ludicrous nature of her venture, she knew the idea would worm away at her until she'd checked it out thoroughly. Besides, she comforted herself, the exercise would be good for getting her back into condition.

The shopping complex on the far end of town had been abandoned for close to three years, victim of the economic downturn.

The weedy asphalt surface was riddled with fissures, the empty buildings standing like ghostly sentinels against the stormy sky.

Ivy hugged her jacket around her as the rain pattered down, making oil-slicked puddles on the ground. The space was hemmed in by a thick border of trees and shrubs, hugging the periphery of the parking area like a leafy green scarf. After a moment to reconnoiter, she headed off toward the far end of the lot, in the direction of a dilapidated trailer.

The rain came down with increasing intensity, snaking under her hood and down her back. Quickening her pace, she half jogged, half slid across the slick asphalt. She was disappointed to find the collection bins had been removed, leaving only a dilapidated trailer to mark the spot where the recycling center had been. The paint was chipped and irregular, but Ivy could just make out the words *Cash for Cans* in flaky white paint. The back-end trailer door had been torn away, leaving a yawning empty hole. The interior was completely dark.

Though she leaned in and strained her eyes, she could not see clear to the back. The intense darkness made goose bumps prickle her skin. She checked her cell phone again; still no messages from Tim. "Come on, Ivy," she scolded herself. "Quit being a chicken. You've got to figure this thing out while there's still a chance for Moe."

Sucking in a deep breath, she climbed up onto the rusted metal threshold and stepped into the trailer.

The air had a moldy, damp smell, and the place where her fingers touched metal was clammy to the touch. Wishing desperately that she had brought her flashlight, she made her way inch by inch toward the back. A tiny window at the far end let in just enough light for her to make out a pile of rubbish, half-mashed cardboard boxes and stacks of newspaper.

She crept forward as the rain exploded against the metal roof. The sound made her ears ring. A distant rumble of thunder echoed oddly in the musty chamber. A few steps closer and she'd reached the pile of debris. The closest box that was relatively intact lay on its side, one flap open on the soggy floor.

With the tip of her foot she slid the other side open.

Something shot out of the box and grazed her leg. She screamed and fell back, the damp cold penetrating the seat of her jeans. Frantically, she crab-walked backward, away from the thing.

Heart still hammering, she got to her feet. Whatever had careened out of the box was now sitting on the top of the pile, looking at her with luminous yellow eyes.

A small cat no bigger than her work glove peered at her.

She tried to get her lungs started again. "Man, you scared me, kitty."

The cat calmly groomed itself. Ivy poked halfheartedly at the rest of the pile, finding nothing other than soggy newspapers and bits of broken glass. Chiding herself for indulging her silly idea, she gave up her search and turned to go. The cat gave a plaintive mew.

"I guess it's pretty lonely here, huh? And cold." Ivy took out the packet her mother had given her and opened the foil. She put it on a dry spot on the floor. The cat jumped down at once and began to nibble delicately.

Ivy wondered where the cat had come from. It didn't behave as though it was feral. She'd probably been dumped in the field by some callous pet owner who believed cats could survive just fine without a home. The little animal had at least found shelter, but her fur hung loose on her starved frame. Ivy thought of Moe alone and fending for himself in a strange and hostile world.

When the cat finished, Ivy held out her hands. "I can't promise you red beans and rice every night, but you can bunk at my place if you want. At least it's dry."

The cat cocked her head for a moment as if considering the offer and then allowed Ivy to pick her up. She tucked the almost weightless creature into her jacket pocket, feeling its rib bones protruding against her fingers as she did so. "Come on, kitty. Let's get out of this smelly place."

Outside, the sky had grown even darker, the rain continuing to fall. She headed for the trees, hoping to at least stick to some kind of cover until she got back out onto the main road.

She'd made it several yards when she caught a glimpse of him.

If the man hadn't had such pale blond hair, she might not have seen him at all, dressed in dark colors, tucked in the shadow of a massive fir.

He was far enough away that she couldn't see his face. It didn't matter. She knew it was him—the man with the magazine.

Though he didn't move at first, she could feel his eyes burning into her. Slowly he reached into his pocket and began to inch toward her.

Ivy's entire body felt shot through with paralyzing cold. After a moment of frozen panic, she took off, ducking low, running under the trees and toward the main road. It was too risky to stop and try to call for help. The man would surely catch her if she tried.

He started to run when she did. His feet crunched through the wet grass. He was close, so close she could hear his harsh breathing. The panic spiraled out of control as she felt his hand on her back, reaching, trying to grasp her by the jacket. When his fingers got a hold she whirled and kicked out as hard as she could. Her foot caught him in the stomach.

He grunted and went down on one knee. She didn't hesitate, but ran again, as fast as she dared across the uneven ground.

Her feet slipped on the soaked grass, sending her crashing into a prickly shrub. She fought her way out, ignoring the distressed mew from inside her jacket. Why in the world had she come to such a desolate spot in the first place?

There was no time to indulge in recrimination as she ran. Her breath came in pants and her shoulder began to ache. Another hundred yards and she would make it to the road, but then what? What if there was no one to help? It was not a well-traveled street.

She didn't dare stop as she pressed her head down and sprinted as fast as she could manage.

A noise from in front made her stop short, her feet skidding. Ears straining, she listened. Another snap of branches underfoot confirmed her fears. How had he gotten ahead of her? Had he circled around the other way to cut her off before she reached the road?

Her heart hammered so hard it sent shudders through her

body. She didn't know whether to try to run around him or head back the other way. The thought of heading even deeper into the woods terrified her.

She scanned in every direction, raindrops momentarily blinding her. Maybe she should risk stopping to call for help.

Ahead and to the right was a thick clump of thistles, rising in thorny splendor. If she could conceal herself there for just a minute, long enough to make one call…

After a moment more she bent low and skirted around the giant clump of green.

Fingers shaking with cold and fear she dialed. Pressing the phone to her ear, she tried to peer through the thorny branches. She was horrified to discover her phone wasn't receiving a signal. She was cut off from help of any kind.

Her mind whirled with possibilities. Go back? Go ahead? Stay put and hope he didn't find her?

None of the options sounded good. Several yards ahead came the sound of feet pushing through the wet grass. The sounds grew closer and closer until she was galvanized into action. She bolted from behind her screen and tried to circle wide enough to have a clear shot to the road.

It wasn't enough.

She heard a grunt of surprise and the figure pursued her.

"Stop," he called.

Ivy put a hand more firmly around the cat and ran as fast as she was able until her feet hit a patch of mud. She went down on her back, fingers still cradled around the cat, the wind knocked out of her.

Her pursuer was upon her.

Rain streamed into her face as she tried to turn over and get her legs underneath her again. Blinded by the water that coursed into her eyes, Ivy knew that she would not surrender easily. If he did kill her, it would be the hardest thing he ever did in his life.

Hands gripped her shoulders.

She screamed.

TWENTY

He grasped her arms tightly, trying to understand her fear.

"Let go of me," she hissed.

"Ivy? Ivy, are you hurt?" He looked down into her face. His wet hair dripped water onto her forehead as he knelt in front of her.

She stared at him, gasping. "Tim? Is it you?"

"Are you all right? What happened?" He looked frantically at her, searching for signs of injury. Something, anything, that would explain the terror in her eyes. "What is going on? Why were you running?"

She sat up and fell into his arms, crying, hiccupping and laughing all at the same time. He held her gently, as if she were made of delicate ice crystals, pressing his warm cheek to her forehead. He exhaled. Whatever it was, he could handle it, as long as she was safe.

"It's okay, Ivy. It's okay now. Whatever happened, it's over." He took off his jacket and wrapped it around her shoulders, chafing her arms to warm her.

"A man. There." She stabbed a finger behind her. "He tried to grab me, but I kicked him. He was following me earlier. I saw him in town this morning, too."

Tim stared. "He's out there?"

She nodded.

He felt an anger stir in his gut. "Stay here," he commanded.

She grabbed his wrist. "No, Tim. He's dangerous. Don't go."

He squeezed her fingers. "Just stay here."

He ran as stealthily as he could, through the soggy mess of trees and grass. There was no sign of the man. He wanted to keep looking, find him and yank an explanation out of him the hard way, but he was afraid to leave Ivy for much longer.

He returned to her and put a hand under her elbow to help her up. "I don't see anyone. Just in case he's still there, let's move. Are you okay to walk?"

"I think so."

In spite of her words, her legs were shaking so badly that Tim picked her up and made his way hastily to the spot along the side of the road where he'd parked his truck.

When the engine was on and the heater running full blast he turned to face her, trying to tamp down the anger that hummed in his veins. "What is going on? Unfortunately I was in a meeting so it took me a while to get your message. It was something about the recycling center but I didn't understand it. I came as fast as I could."

Her cheeks pinked. "It was a stupid idea. I thought about the Cannery Row reference and how Cyril ran the recycling shack for a while. I thought maybe he'd left something here."

"Ah, the cans. I get it. It makes sense in a weird sort of way." He turned a stern face to her. "But, Ivy, coming out here on your own? You could have been killed. That guy, whoever he was, isn't some upstanding citizen and he's connected to Cyril's murder somehow. That was reckless and you should have known better. You're trained in risk assessment and all that, aren't you? What were you thinking?"

"I know, I know. It was stupid."

"Yes, it was." He turned the heating vents to direct warmth to her side.

She was convulsed by shivering, her teeth chattering. "I'm sorry."

"You should be. When I saw you there, running, I thought... Well, I don't know what I thought." He cleared his throat and tried to get his feelings under control. "Don't ever do that again, Beria."

She laughed. "I think I can safely promise that. There is one good thing that came out of this, you know."

"And what is that?"

She pulled out the tiny cat and put her on the seat. "I got to perform a rescue."

Tim looked from the cat to Ivy and back to the cat again. He laughed, the joy he always felt at being near her amplified by the thought of what could have happened. "You are one in a million."

"I hope you mean that in a good way."

"You know I do."

He didn't dare look at her as they pulled out onto the road. She did not want him, this amazing, exceptional woman. She'd made it clear, and it was getting too hard to hide it. He knew that when the crazy episode was over, he would have to let go of her for good. He could not fall in love with a woman who didn't want him. He'd thought things might change when she'd opened her heart to the Lord. He'd been wrong. The pain of it lodged in his gut.

Tim took her back to her home. He went to Moe's apartment to put on dry clothes while she cleaned up. Then he let himself back into her place and rummaged around the kitchen.

He set to work cooking two grilled cheese sandwiches and opening a can of tuna for the cat that crouched, tail swishing. The cat lapped up the fish with a tiny pink tongue.

"Hope you don't mind grilled cheese for dinner. Your refrigerator is a little low on supplies. It was either grilled cheese or a half jar of pickle relish."

She slid into a chair and watched as Tim maneuvered around the kitchen. "Grilled cheese sounds perfect to me." Ivy saw the cat look up from her dinner and stare at them with golden eyes. "I see you've pleased the feline customer."

He smiled. "I'm a dog person actually, but she turned her nose up when I offered Milk-Bones and the idea of playing fetch doesn't seem to appeal to her so we went with tuna. What are you going to name her?"

"I'm not sure yet. I'm going to go with Cat for the moment."

"Catchy, no pun intended." Tim joined her and they munched the crispy, golden sandwiches.

"Any word on Moe?" she asked around a cheesy bite.

He didn't want to tell her. She'd been through so much already. "Indirectly."

She straightened. "Really? What? Tell me."

"I talked to Detective Greenly this morning. It seems a certain gas-station attendant returned from his fishing trip. He says Moe stopped by early Thursday morning and looked through all the Oregon maps on his display shelf."

"Did he say anything about where he was going?"

"No. He asked only one question."

Ivy's eyebrows lifted. "What?"

"He asked if there was electricity in the mountains."

"The mountains? If he headed to the mountains, he could be anywhere."

Tim grimaced at the despair in her voice. "I know. It doesn't help us narrow things down."

Ivy groaned. "Oh, Tim. I'm so worried about Moe. He's got to be scared."

"I am, too. The more we search, the farther away he seems to get. I keep going over the bits we know, the info about Medsci and Roger Smalley. The answer is there somewhere, I'm sure of it."

"And you have an idea, don't you?"

He shrugged. "It's a wild theory, really."

"Could it be wilder than my Cannery Row idea?"

He laughed. "No, you take the cake with that one. I've been doing some research on experimental drugs and there have been a few cases where corporate spies get their hands on research information and sell it to the highest bidder."

"I had no idea."

"Me, neither."

"Do you think Roger was selling info?"

Tim stifled a yawn. "I'm not sure, but what if he was? And what if Cyril stumbled onto the information and passed it to Moe before he was murdered? He did have those medical journals Moe tried to burn. Could be he was trying to figure out how much his stolen info was worth."

"Could he have been murdered by the people buying Roger Smalley's information?"

He shrugged. "I told you it was a wild theory."

"After all that's happened, nothing sounds wild to me anymore."

The clock above the gas fireplace chimed.

Ivy flopped back on the sofa. "What a day. I feel like a deflated balloon."

Taking the cue, Tim hauled himself up. "It's getting late. I'd better go. I'll see you in the morning."

Ivy followed him to the door. "Busy tomorrow?"

"No way. I'm sticking by you, Beria. I can't have you wandering all over creation, rescuing cats and getting into all manner of scrapes." He brushed a strand of hair from her forehead, fingers lingering for a moment on her skin. *Back off, Tim,* his mind said. He wished he could convince his heart to do the same.

Roger Smalley did not look right in the Jaguar, Nick thought.

Some men wore the trappings of luxury with ease, as if they were born to it. Smalley sat in the machine as if it were a camel, uneasily clinging to the steering wheel with fat fingers.

Sad, really, Nick thought as he settled into the passenger seat, inhaling the sweet smell of leather and ignoring the pain in his stomach where the girl had kicked him. A car like this one should be owned with confidence. He tried to discern if the supple leather was actually black or the deepest shade of green.

The rain pattered on the windshield. Idly, Nick wondered if the girl had seen him in the woods closely enough to identify him. He didn't think so with the storm unloading over their heads. It was turning out to be harder than he anticipated keeping track of her comings and goings, even with help.

Smalley glanced over again at Nick, his fingers twitching. "Are you listening? I won't tolerate it, the attention from the police and these so-called friends of somebody named Cyril. I worked too hard and too long to jeopardize my career. I'm done, do you hear me? Done."

Nick let him finish, admiring the smooth lines of the dashboard. "You're obligated to finish the deal."

Smalley blinked several times, a flush creeping over his fleshy face. "I'm not obligated to do anything. You don't own me."

"How fast?"

Smalley blinked again. "What?"

"How fast have you gone?" He pointed to the speedometer.

"I don't know." Smalley's tone was icy. "I keep to the speed limit."

"Shame. That's like having a racehorse and never letting it run."

Smalley huffed impatiently. "Listen, I've got to go. It's been peachy working with you, but it's over. Just tell your boss I'm not doing any more business with him."

Nick peered closely at the sound system. "I don't tell him what to do."

"Fine. Then I'll tell him myself. Get out."

The words were bold but Nick did not miss the tremble of the man's sweaty upper lip. "Suit yourself." He slid out of the plush seat and closed the door. It hardly made a sound.

Smalley drove off at a respectable speed.

"Shame," Nick said aloud.

TWENTY-ONE

He was not pleased. Nick could tell by the tiny lines around his mouth.

The man had come to the boss's place of business, violated an unspoken agreement. Now he sat there on the delicate brocade chair, sweating like a hard-ridden horse.

"You should not have come here, Mr. Smalley." His boss's tone was mild. "It was unwise."

"Unwise? This whole business was unwise. I can't believe I ever got into this deal. What was I thinking?"

"I imagine," he said after a sip of tea, "you were thinking about the car you would buy and the down payment on a three-bedroom home in Aspen."

Nick smiled.

Smalley jerked as if he'd been slapped. "How did you know about Aspen?"

"It doesn't matter. What does matter is that you promised me two formulas and you have only delivered one. That is unfinished business. That is unacceptable. Tea?"

Smalley ignored the question. "I can't take any more risks with all the attention lately. I've given you all I can."

He stirred his cup with a silver spoon. "I promised my buyers two formulas."

"You've got smart people in your country, don't you? They can take the first one and run with it."

How could such a stupid man wind up with a Jaguar? Nick wondered.

"That is not the point," his boss continued. "You have been paid handsomely for two products and you have only delivered one. That makes you, forgive me for saying it, a welcher."

Smalley stared at him. He began to laugh with such vigor it set his jowls wobbling. "A welcher? This isn't a schoolyard game. A welcher, that's a good one. Sticks and stones and all that. I gave you what I could and I'm not going to give you the rest. I can't afford to now that the police are involved and that girl is sniffing around."

"My employee is handling that."

"Really? And just who is this Cyril they kept asking me about? I've never met him. What does he have to do with our deal?"

Nick shifted slightly.

"Again, that is not your concern."

"You're right, it isn't. Nothing about this business concerns me anymore. The deal is off." Smalley rose and walked over to the table. He peered at the collection of knives arranged neatly on the table, next to the almost-finished specimen. "I've never met a taxidermist before. Is this what you do for a hobby?"

"Among other things."

"Weird." He checked his watch.

Nick cleared his throat. "Going somewhere?"

Smalley gave him a quick glance. "No, nowhere. I just came in person to tell you and your boss to leave me alone and stay out of my car."

The boss put his teacup on the table. "Are you sure you can't be persuaded to change your mind? For both our interests?"

"No. I'm pretty certain once I decide on something. I've always been the decisive kind." Smalley smiled and extended his hand. "It was great while it lasted."

Nick walked Smalley to the door.

"Can I buy you guys some breakfast?" Smalley said. "I don't want to leave any bad blood behind. Café across the street says they've got the state's fluffiest pancakes."

Nick didn't answer.

"No, thank you, Roger. Enjoy your meal."

Smalley left and the boss excused himself for a moment.

While he waited, Nick absentmindedly massaged the fingers on his left hand. They remained partially numb after the beating that had changed both his life and his father's. He pictured clearly, the man's face who had wielded the club, blank, impassive.

The man's expression was the same when he finally tracked him down twelve years later.

"Remember me?"

The man blinked, eyes slightly rheumy. "No."

"You beat me when you were shaking down my father for protection money."

"Oh." More blinking. "Yes, I think I do remember that. Your father should have paid. Would've been easier. So, you've come to kill me?"

"Yes."

He shrugged. "Do it then. Don't drag things out, makes it too untidy. Always remember that."

He did remember and it made him irate that things were untidy now. He walked to the window and watched Smalley cross the street to the tiny café, in search of his fluffy pancakes. The sun had broken through the clouds, lending a brilliant cast to the still-wet road. Smalley ran a hand over the sleek lines of his green Jaguar as he passed by, perhaps wicking away a drop of water left on the shining hood.

His boss spoke from the doorway. "You know what to do."

Tim and Ivy stopped in Detective Greenly's cramped office in between search assignments. He was chewing gum for all he was worth. "We checked Smalley out. Nothing that directly connects him to any wrongdoing. As far as Medsci is concerned, he's a glowing employee," Greenly said.

Ivy sighed. "Hmm. I sure would have pegged him for being guilty of something."

He blew a bubble. It popped with a loud crack. "You know what they say. If it walks like a duck…"

Tim raised an eyebrow. "You have the same feeling about him we did?"

"He's living well. Very well. Nice car, nice house." Greenly drumrolled two pencils on the desk.

"I'm sure he earns a good living from Medsci," Ivy said.

"I'm sure he does, but last year he purchased a home in Aspen and spent three weeks on the French Riviera."

Tim laughed. "Wow. I spent my vacation putting up drywall. Clearly I'm in the wrong line of work."

Ivy chuckled. She remembered the drywall project. He hadn't been able to straighten his back for a week. "So where do we go from here?"

"We don't go anywhere. You two can stick to the search for Moe. I've got someone looking into Smalley's background and watching the airport."

Ivy watched the detective blow another bubble. "Why the airport?"

"Smalley bought a one-way ticket to Portugal. His flight leaves tonight."

She stiffened. "If he runs, we may never figure out the mystery."

"We're on it, Ms. Beria. The police are handling that end of things. Just do me a favor and call me if you see Smalley. He's currently on vacation from work and not answering his home phone or cell. I don't have enough people to put someone on him exclusively."

They stood to leave.

Greenly spit out the gum and shoved another stick into his mouth. "There's one other thing."

Ivy noticed an uneasy cast to his face. "What is it?"

"County Search and Rescue is pulling the plug."

She gasped. "What? How can they stop searching when Moe is still out there somewhere?"

"Purely a numbers game, Ivy, you know that. They're needed elsewhere. It's summer-vacation season and they've got plenty of disoriented tourists to find."

Her heart sank. "Oh, no. How will we tell Madge they're giving up on him?"

Greenly shook his head. "It's terrible. Being in the business, you know that resources have to be spread out for the greater good." His eyes filled with compassion. "I've got a kid myself and I can't imagine hearing that news. I don't want to give up on Moe and we'll continue to do what we can, but…"

"I know, I know."

Tim wrapped an arm around her. "We'll keep looking, Ivy. Our luck's got to change sooner or later."

She bit her lip to keep in a sigh. "When are you going to tell Madge about County?"

"I'll stop over there tomorrow morning. They're going to give it one more day."

Tim nodded. "We'll be there when you tell her."

"Okay. I've got work to do. You two kids stay out of trouble."

Ivy and Tim stepped out into the humid morning.

"Where should we start?" Tim asked.

"I don't know anymore." Ivy hunched down into the front seat of Tim's truck. "This searching is getting us nowhere. It's just so frustrating."

Tim consulted his mother's list. "Moe's uncle took him up to Lake Soway last spring. That's about an hour east of here. Are you game?"

She nodded without enthusiasm. "I guess so."

He patted her knee. "How about I stop at the grocery and get us some snacks to take along?"

Though she didn't feel the least bit hungry, she knew what he was trying to do. "Sure. Sounds good."

He drove to a small strip of stores on the edge of town. She stayed in the truck, watching the clouds morph from one odd shape to the next. Was Moe looking at the same thing? Had he been able to find shelter from the storm? She felt the stirring again, the bitter sting of being unable to rescue him.

Her eyes wandered over the people coming and going, steeped in the business of their own lives. Would she feel happily oblivious if she was back on the line, steeped in hers? A man with a shiny bald head came out of the tiny post office and made his way to the ATM machine. Ivy sat bolt upright.

Roger Smalley.

Tim got in. "Just to cheer you up, I got us some chocolate-chip cookies, too."

She pulled his arm. "Look, by the ATM. It's Smalley."

The man pulled some cash out of the machine. Even from a distance it looked like a thick stack.

Tim was already dialing the phone. "It's Greenly's voice mail." He left a quick message and hung up. They watched Smalley pocket his cash and slide into the Jaguar.

Tim started the engine and waited until the car pulled out into traffic before he fell in behind him.

"What are you doing? Greenly said we weren't supposed to get involved."

Tim didn't take his eyes off the car ahead of them. "I'm not involved. I'm going to find out where he's headed and dutifully report it to the detective."

She grinned. "You're getting pretty bold in your old age."

He gave her a huge grin. "Must be the company I'm keeping."

Her heart sped up.

They followed at a discreet distance, leaving the town behind them. Smalley took a side road, which gradually ascended. He kept the Jaguar to a precise thirty-five miles an hour.

"Where is he headed?" Ivy shaded her eyes as they drove into the sun.

"I don't know unless..." Tim's brows drew together in thought.

"What?"

"The private airport."

"It's so small, only one strip. Wouldn't he head for the international to catch a flight to Portugal?"

"Not if he's being cagey."

Ivy tried dialing Greenly's number again with no better result. As they rounded a turn, Tim had to brake suddenly when a deer bounded across the road. Fortunately, the motorbike behind them slowed, too.

When Tim started around the corner again, the Jaguar was nowhere in sight.

Ivy leaned forward. "He must be around the next turn."

Tim sped up as much as was safe until Smalley's car was once again in their sight.

"Whew." Ivy straightened. "I thought we'd lost him."

Tim wiggled his eyebrows. "Just call me The Shadow."

Without warning the Jaguar sped up.

"He must have spotted us."

Tim increased speed. "Are we that recognizable?"

"He's being cagey, remember?"

She gripped the dashboard as the truck took a sharp curve. "Keep on him."

"I'll try, but if he speeds up much more I'm going to have to let him go."

Ivy opened her mouth to respond when her words were stopped by a horrific explosion. As Smalley accelerated, the back of his car blew apart in a shower of flame and twisted metal. It shot off the road, down the embankment.

Fighting to keep the truck under control as bits of metal rained down on the windshield, Tim pulled to the side. Ivy grabbed the fire extinguisher and they both took off, slipping and sliding down the slope toward the wreck.

The car was topside down, the front smashed into an unyielding tree. The passenger window was so badly twisted there was no room to pull the victim out. The only hope of rescue was the door. She saw Tim use the tire iron he'd grabbed from the truck to try to pry open the hot metal.

Ivy noted the flames growing higher and higher. The heat was intense as she tried in vain to quench the flames. It was useless. Tongues of fire continued to pour out the window.

She grabbed Tim's arm to drag him away.

"I've almost got it," he yelled, yanking at the door, sweat pouring down his face.

The flames licked closer and closer to the gas tank.

"No," she screamed, pulling him. "It's too late."

They both staggered away as the car exploded in an enormous angry fireball, the force pushing them to their knees.

Gasping for breath, Ivy and Tim watched in horrified silence as the flames continued to devour the car and its occupant.

Tim swallowed hard. "I guess Mr. Smalley's not going to be making that flight after all."

Nick pulled the motorbike to the shoulder, idling for a moment in the glare from the burning wreck.

He watched the sleek car blister and pucker, its sides blackening and twisting in the intense heat.

"Shame," he said, over the crack of the fire.

TWENTY-TWO

It took a half hour for Detective Greenly to arrive at the accident scene. The afternoon sun bathed the woods in long shadow. Ivy and Tim sat on a fallen tree as the detective unwrapped his last stick of gum.

"Are you sure he didn't crash, then explode?"

Tim nodded vigorously. "Very sure. As soon as he accelerated, bam. The thing just disintegrated."

"What a waste of a fine automobile." Greenly watched his officer photograph the scene from every possible angle. He shook his head. "Sometimes this job is the worst."

Ivy shivered as a wind swirled through the pine needles above their heads. "Can we go now?"

He cracked his gum thoughtfully. "Yes, but don't do any more investigating. Stick to finding Moe."

She nodded, allowing Tim to guide her back to the truck.

He signaled for a turn.

"No, keep going. We've got to check out Lake Soway."

He raised an eyebrow. "You're sure? Wouldn't you rather go home?"

"Yes, I would, but it's even more important now that we find Moe before the bad guys do."

He gritted his teeth. "You're right. Let's hit it."

Lake Soway was lovely, a crystal-clear oblong of water providing entertainment to swimmers, boaters and kids on inner tubes. They hiked the steep trail around the water, checking with everyone who would talk to them, with no luck.

Hot and tired, they drove back toward town into a brilliant sherbet sunset. Neither one of them spoke but Ivy knew they'd both hoped to give Madge good news. Instead they headed to the apartment complex in somber silence until Ivy's cell phone rang.

"Hey, V. Where are you?"

"Hi, Mitch. Heading home finally."

"So late? Where have you been all day? I tried to call earlier but there was no answer."

"Searching for Moe and before that, dealing with the police. Someone blew up Roger Smalley's car."

"Smalley? The guy you think is connected to Cyril somehow?"

"Yes."

There was a long silence.

"Someone blew up his car?"

"Into smithereens."

Another silence.

"Mitch? Are you still there?"

"Yeah, yeah. I'm here."

"You okay?"

"Uh-huh."

"Still helping with the search?"

"Yeah, why? Did you and Tim find any leads on his whereabouts?"

"No, we still have no clue. We'll be at Madge's in the morning."

"Oh, okay. See you tomorrow."

Ivy thought she heard a strange note of relief in her cousin's voice before he disconnected.

Tim glanced at her. "Is Mitch staying out of trouble?"

She closed the phone thoughtfully. "I wish I knew."

The next morning, Ivy said goodbye to Cat after filling her bowl and checking the baking pan she'd turned into an impromptu kitty litter box. Tim hugged Ivy before they got into the truck. She leaned into his chest, wishing they could avoid adding to Madge's pain by telling her the official searchers had given up on her son. Ivy inhaled the scent of soap and snuggled her head under his chin.

When she finally took a deep breath and settled herself in the truck she felt sad at the loss of his touch. She wished they could drive away, to some warm sunny spot and leave all the trouble behind them. Starting over. It sounded so good. *It's been a trying time, Ivy. Don't turn to mush.*

She diverted her mind to trying to think of positive things to say to Madge. Mitch was already there when they pulled up.

Madge greeted them with a hopeful look. "Any news? Did you find anything? Anything at all?"

"No, Madge, but we haven't given up," Ivy said, holding her hand.

"Maybe they'll find him tomorrow." Her look traveled over the three of them. "Where will they look? What areas?"

They were spared from having to answer her when the detective arrived and broke the news that the official search had ended.

Madge blinked several times and sank into a chair. Ivy thought she was going to burst into tears but she composed herself enough to thank the detective. "God will provide for my Moe. He'll help him find his way back, I know it. I appreciate all the time those searchers put in. Now at least we know where not to look for him, right?"

"Right. That's a good way to look at it." Greenly gave her a sympathetic look and excused himself. "I've got to go to Salem overnight. Can you two stay out of trouble until I get back?"

Tim laughed as they walked the detective to his car. "We'll try."

Madge had the phone pressed to her ear when they returned. Her expression was a mixture of wonder and disbelief.

Ivy could imagine only one thing that would put such a smile on the woman's face. "Is it Moe?"

Madge nodded so hard the curls flapped against her forehead.

"Where is he? Is he all right?" The words tumbled out of Ivy's mouth.

"He says he's okay. Don't hang up, Moe, honey. Tell Mama where you are. Please…"

She lowered the phone slowly. "He hung up before he told me his location."

"What did he say? Anything that would be a clue?" Tim said, after he hugged her.

"No, no. He said he's been watching his shows and eating graham crackers. He loves those. He rambled a bit. Nothing concrete."

"Did the number come up on your caller ID?"

"It just said 'out of area.'" Her eyes misted. "Oh, I'm so relieved that he's okay. I just know he's somewhere close. I can feel it. He sounded so happy."

Mitch double-checked the phone. "Yes, it does say 'out of area.'" He blew out a breath. "How can this kid be so hard to find?"

Ivy felt a mixture of relief and frustration at being connected so briefly to the man they simply couldn't locate. She sat next to Madge and held her hand while she cried, fighting to keep the tears out of her own eyes. "Tell me again what he said, every word."

Madge went through everything she could remember. "Oh, wait. He did say something about church chairs. He's always liked to count the chairs at Cornerstone." She blushed. "That's really why we switched from your church, Tim. Moe couldn't stand the pews. I figured if he wouldn't even sit down there was no hope of hearing the message. But he couldn't be there. Someone would have found him for sure."

Ivy frowned. "And why would he need to snatch a motor scooter and look at maps to get there?"

"We should check it out anyway. Closest church first." Mitch stood to go. "Let's move before the trail gets cold."

Ivy eyed him. "It just doesn't make sense."

Mitch snorted. "Maybe not, but do you have any better ideas?"

She had to admit she didn't. They said goodbye to Madge and headed for the oldest church in town, a clapboard-sided building covered by a brilliant wash of green ivy. A prechurch choir practice was under way. The director took a break to come and talk to them.

"Moe used to come in every Saturday morning to watch us set up the chairs for service. He could tell me without even counting how many we'd put out." He took off his glasses and polished them. "He's some kind of genius. I haven't seen him recently, though."

They chatted for a bit and he returned to the choir. The three prowled the property, stopping in the library. Ivy flipped through a scrapbook with photos from a year's worth of church events. A cheerful woman in a pink pantsuit insisted they take it after she heard about their mission. "We try to photograph everyone at our major events. Maybe it will help with the investigation somehow."

Tim thanked her and they left. The sunlight dazzled their eyes as they stood in the parking lot to reconnoiter.

Tim folded his arms across his chest. "Where to now?"

"Well," Mitch began after a pause, "Moe could have been talking about another church. Maybe one from a neighboring town, say?"

Ivy sighed. "Oh, man. There are three right here in our town plus six in Centerville and four that I know of in Brubaker."

"Looks like we've got our day planned then."

"Okay." Mitch fumbled for keys. "Let's split up. I'll take Centerville and the south end here. You two take the north end and Brubaker."

Ivy felt a new hopefulness course through her body. "Sounds good. We'll meet back at my apartment for dinner. I'll spring for pizza."

Mitch waved and drove away.

"He sure is determined," Tim said with a puzzled look.

"Yeah." They fell into silence as they set off in search of the nearest church.

Three hours and two stops later they pulled up at the Loving Hands Church in Brubaker. The day had progressed to swelter-ing and Ivy's shirt stuck to her body. They found the elderly pastor on a stepladder trying to repair the sign outside the front door.

Tim hustled over and grabbed the heavy board, which threatened to slip out of the man's hands. He looked up in surprise, round cheeks flushed pink. "Well, hello. I was hoping God would send me a helping hand and here you are."

Tim introduced them and changed places with the pastor on the ladder. He set to work nailing the sign securely in place. Ivy and the pastor watched.

"That's a good fellow you've got there," the man said.

Ivy blushed. "Oh, he's not really…" She swallowed. "Yes, he's a real good fellow."

The pastor insisted they partake of some ice water. He led them inside the tiny church. Ivy and Tim sagged in disappointment. Shiny wood pews filled the small space instead of chairs.

The pastor gave them a questioning look and Ivy explained their mission. He raised an eyebrow. "Oh, yes. I believe I met the boy you're talking about."

Ivy coughed on a sip of water. "Really? Recently?"

"No, I remember him from an all-county church retreat, I think. Loves numbers, right?"

Tim nodded. "Yes, that's Moe."

The man laughed. "I remember. I told him he'd be a great pastor because he'd remember every page, chapter and verse he ever read."

Though she knew it was hopeless, Ivy asked the question anyway. "But you haven't seen him in the past week?"

"I'm sorry, no. I will definitely let you know if I do."

They thanked him and returned to the truck.

The pastor leaned his head in the open window. "I'll pray for Moe. God has a way of bringing home lost souls."

Lost souls.

Ivy felt a jolt of realization. For the first time in a very long time, she did not feel adrift. In spite of being removed from her profession, and the worry about Moe, she reveled in a peace that she couldn't have imagined. It was too incredible to comprehend. He'd finally brought her lost soul home, kicking and screaming all the way.

She looked over at Tim. His warm smile told her he was thinking the very same thing.

Tim propped his feet up on the ottoman, next to Ivy's. The pizza sat on the coffee table, dripping with cheese, but fatigue outweighed hunger. He tried again to route his mind back to the search.

Cat wandered among them, twisting her tail around their legs.

Mitch reached for a slice of pizza. "This is getting to be a pattern. We search all day with absolutely no results."

Tim closed his eyes, willing the tiredness to retreat long enough for him to think of another place they could look. "At least we know he's all right. That was a pretty big encouragement. We're not searching in vain."

Mitch sighed. "Yeah, well, if he doesn't show up soon he might not stay that way."

Ivy started. "I hate to hear you say that."

He shrugged. "Just worried, that's all. Cyril's dead. Guy blows up in his car. Bad stuff." He finished the last bite of pizza and stretched. "I'm bushed. Can hardly keep my eyes open."

Tim eyed the shadows under Mitch's eyes. "Why don't you bunk in Moe's apartment with me? He's got a futon that would work, I think, if you're not picky."

"At this point, I could sleep standing up." He took the key from Tim. "See you in the morning."

Tim helped pick up the pizza mess. He felt Ivy's eyes on him as he wiped down the counter.

He looked up. "What?"

"I was just thinking what a nice person you are. Helping out the pastor today, and all the things you've done for me."

He tingled at the emotion in her eyes. *Easy, Tim. She's just thanking you. Her position hasn't changed.* "My pleasure. I have enjoyed every minute of your leave from work way more than you have."

"I'm going to miss our time together when I go back."

There it was. The roadblock he was expecting. He put down the towel and came over to her, losing himself for a moment in the intense green of her eyes. He'd give it one more try. One more chance. "Ivy, please consider this. You don't have to have one or the other. Your work doesn't have to be a wall that keeps you away from people…from me."

She looked away from the tenderness in his gaze. "It's an intense job. To do it well, I've got to give it my all. There's no room…"

He put a finger under her chin and directed her face to his. "There is, if you want there to be. Tell me the truth, Ivy. Tell me you don't want me around and I'll accept it. I'll keep my distance and move on."

She felt lost in the shimmer of his eyes. "Tim. I do…I feel…"

He fingered her hair. "You've been through a lot, with Sadie, with Antonio, and that hurt you deeply. I just hope that someday you can let go of those things and find room for me in that heart of yours." He embraced her one more time, praying that it wouldn't be the last.

TWENTY-THREE

The knocking on the door at five thirty didn't awaken Ivy at first, but it woke Cat. She tiptoed around Ivy's face until her eyes finally fluttered open. The knock repeated itself, soft and insistent.

Ivy pulled on some sweats and opened the door to a rumpled Tim. His hair stood up in unruly patches and his eyes were bleary. "Sorry it's so early. I thought of something and I knew you'd want to hear it right away."

She let him in. "You look like you've been awake all night."

"I have. Your cousin snores louder than a freight train."

"Is he still asleep?"

"Can't you hear the walls rattling?"

With a chuckle, she started the coffee and sank down on the chair. "What is the revelation that required you to wake me up at five thirty?"

"Something the pastor said. He mentioned he'd met Moe before at an all-county church retreat."

"Yes." It took a moment before Ivy's mind started to whir. She grabbed the scrapbook from the side table and began to flip through it. "And Cornerstone said they tried to keep photos of every major event. If they participated, maybe there's a picture in here somewhere."

She thumbed through the plastic-covered pages. "I don't see Moe anywhere."

Tim settled in next to her and they both peered at the pages that documented everything from baptisms to blessing of the animals. She stopped at a picture crowded with people all wearing matching bandanas around their necks. "Hang on a second."

She retrieved a magnifying glass from the dresser drawer and trained it over the crowd. "Look. Look right there. Is that Moe?"

He squinted at the page. "I'm not sure. That definitely looks like Madge standing next to him."

Her heart in her throat, Ivy scanned the picture for some sign or notation that would identify the place. "It doesn't say, but it's definitely wooded and that's a mountain peak in the back. Do you suppose?"

"Let's go ask Madge. I know she won't mind being awakened for this."

"Should we tell Mitch?"

"Nah, let him sleep. We can phone him if the lead pans out."

They drove at a good clip over to Madge's house. It was just after six thirty when they knocked softly on her door.

She opened it, wide-eyed, clutching a flowered robe around her middle. "Tim, Ivy. What is it? It isn't…"

Tim reached out a calming hand. "No news, Madge, but we may have stumbled onto a lead. Sorry to come so early, but we just had to ask you something."

"Anything, anything that would help find my Moe. Come in, come in."

Ivy showed her the picture. "Is that you and Moe, Madge?" She held her breath while Madge held the picture close to her face.

The woman's eyes narrowed then widened. She dropped the book in her lap. "Yes, yes, that's Moe. I forgot all about that trip. We went to a county church retreat last year up at Sugar Pine."

"Where exactly is Sugar Pine? Is it close?"

"About three hours north. It's a few cabins and a field where people can pitch tents." Her eyes rolled in thought. "And there is a meeting hall where we worshipped and they set up rows and rows of chairs. Moe was so excited. They even had a little TV so he could watch his episodes."

Tim sat on the edge of his seat. "Would Moe know how to get there?"

"I don't think so. He doesn't pay attention to directions when we're driving."

Ivy crumpled in her chair.

"But if he saw the route on a map…" Tim started.

Madge beamed and clasped her hands together. "Then he could memorize a path to the moon."

The three of them stared at one another until Madge burst into a shower of tears. "Oh, my stars. Could it be? Could he be there?"

Tim squeezed her hand. "Madge, let's be as calm as we can. This is a long shot but it fits with what you heard from him on the phone." He looked at Ivy with an unspoken question.

"Of course we'll drive up right now and check it out," she said. "Will you call Detective Greenly's office and leave a message about our plan?"

"Yes, yes, I will. And I'll stay right here by this phone and wait for your call. Be careful, and thank you."

They left her dabbing a pink tissue to her eyes. Ivy glanced in the back of the truck to make sure her pack of gear was still safely stowed. She made sure the radio pager was clipped to her belt, not that it would provide any kind of assistance. It made her feel better knowing it was there.

Tim pulled onto the road and headed out of town.

Ivy could not keep down the excitement that bubbled in her gut. "Sugar Pine has to be the place. It's in the mountains, they've got chairs and he looked at maps at the gas station."

"I want to believe it, too, but we need to take it one step at a time."

She smiled. "Always the voice of reason."

"Somebody has to be."

"Ha-ha. Get the lead out, Carnelli, and let's go rescue Moe."

"So much for taking it one step at a time."

Tim stopped at a small mini-mart to buy graham crackers and water and fill up the truck.

Ivy was stunned when Antonio pulled up next to Tim's truck. He flashed her a dazzling smile and walked over to the open window.

"Hey, Ivy. Fancy running into you here. The guys and I are going fishing. Wanna come?"

"No, Antonio." She marveled again at how handsome he was, how fit. The epitome of a hero.

He touched her hand where it lay on the window frame. "Come on, Ivy. We used to have all kinds of fun together. I miss that."

"I'm sure you're not lacking for company."

He grimaced. "All right, I deserved that. I was an idiot to walk out of your life. We had great times together and I just kinda freaked out when I felt like you were pushing me toward something more."

She didn't answer.

"But that's no reason we can't be friends again." He stroked her fingers and bent to press his lips to them. "Best friends."

She stared at him, taking in the perfect features, the boyish charm. Suddenly she felt as if she'd slipped on a pair of glasses that brought everything into crisp focus. Antonio wasn't a bad guy. He'd never promised her anything but fun. Now, for some reason she couldn't articulate, fun was not enough. "You know, Antonio, friends are people who take all of you—the good and the bad and the angsty. I think I need that kind of friend now."

He cocked an eyebrow. "So you're giving me the brush-off?"

She smiled. "Think of it as being canceled on the way to a fire."

"I hate that."

She laughed. "Me, too, but there's always another fire right around the corner."

He gave her a kiss on the cheek. "Bye, Ivy."

"Goodbye, Antonio."

Tim returned with an armful of groceries. Ivy knew he'd been stalling returning to the car, to give her time to converse with Antonio.

"He seems to find you everywhere," Tim said as he started the engine. He made a show of adjusting the side mirrors. "Did you make any plans with him?"

"No. Now let's get moving."

He smiled and pulled out onto the road.

An hour passed and the scenery became mountainous and thick with trees. The shade was a welcome relief from the sizzling sunlight.

She rolled down the window to breathe in the sweet smell of pine and cedar. In spite of the gravity of their mission, Ivy was happy to be sitting next to Tim, sharing the adventure.

What had he said before about finding room in her heart for him? She realized with a start that there had always been a space for him, but she'd kept her feelings confined, enclosed in a place where she could keep it away from the rest of her life, to keep it still and silent. She thought Antonio filled that space, but he hadn't. He'd only distracted her.

It was getting harder and harder to hide from the truth and it scared her. She watched him, feeling an emotion stir in her that warmed her to the core.

"Tim?"

"Yes?"

"I…" She was interrupted by the ring of her cell phone. She answered. "Ivy Beria."

"Where are you?" Mitch's voice charged through the phone. "I woke up and found everyone gone."

"Hi, Mitch. Tim said to tell you, you snore." The reception grew worse as they headed up a steep slope.

"Yeah, yeah. Where are you?"

"I can't hear you very well so I'll make this quick. We think we have a lead on Moe."

She could only make out one word of his reply.

"Where?"

"Sugar Pine Lodge. He went to a church retreat there."

Clicks crackled the line. "Ivy, you've got to turn around and come back."

"What?"

"…come back. He's…"

"Mitch, you're breaking up." She couldn't make out some of the words but Mitch's tone was desperate.

"…watching…to Moe. Turn around."

"I can't understand, Mitch. We'll be back later today. I'll talk to you then." She clicked off the phone.

Tim shot her a quizzical look. "What was that all about?"

"I don't know. He told me to turn around, but I couldn't hear the reason why."

"Do you want to head back and come up here later?"

"With Madge on pins and needles? No way. We've got to finish this thing today."

"That's what I think, too."

Tim had to turn his full attention to driving for the next hour. Ivy noticed how dry the vegetation was in spite of the recent rain, the pockets of grass golden and parched, the pine needles on the ground brittle as glass. It would be a real bad time for a wildfire, she thought.

The road grew windy and narrow at times.

Ivy smiled, thinking of her sister, Sadie, who was notoriously carsick on long trips. Sadie would have gone along anyway on their adventure; nothing could have kept her away. It felt so good to think about her sister without the surge of anger that used to accompany every memory. She thought maybe sometime soon she would read a few of her mother's Penny Pocket stories and see if she could find more of her sister's memories there. She silently thanked the Lord for removing her burden and not turning away from her anger.

Tim risked a glance at her. "What are you thinking about? You look happy."

She shrugged. "Don't know. Enjoying the drive I guess."

"How come I don't hear your radio squawking?"

"I turned it off a few miles back."

He was so surprised he slowed the truck for a moment before continuing. "You did? Why?"

"I guess I wanted to be here fully for a change. With you."

He didn't answer, but she thought she saw a strong emotion wash over his face.

Without warning, a steep graveled path branched off from the main road. They almost missed the small sign that read Sugar Pine Lodge.

"There!" Ivy jabbed a finger at the sign and Tim pulled off. He eased the truck onto a rocky area edged by dry grass and parked.

"Why are you stopping here?"

"If Moe felt he had to run away, he's clearly scared. I think we better try not to frighten him any further."

Ivy grabbed her backpack and Tim carried the bag of graham crackers and water. Together they crept toward the nearest building, hoping for some sign that their hunch had been correct.

Madge's description had been right on. The field for tent camping was covered with tall dry grass, a circle of six cabins forming a perimeter. Tim grabbed her arm suddenly. She barely contained her cry of surprise.

"There," he whispered in her ear. "It's the motor scooter."

Sure enough, the scooter leaned against the side of the smallest cabin. Her heart beat so fast it seemed to vibrate her whole body.

They walked toward the cabin, the only sound coming from the murmur of grass under their feet and the sound of a quickening wind.

After a look from Tim, Ivy cleared her throat. "Moe? Are you in there? It's Ivy, your neighbor."

No movement from the cabin.

"Moe? Your mother sent us. She's very worried about you. We brought some more graham crackers. Are you in there?"

They were on the front porch step. Ivy reached out to turn the door handle when Tim stopped her. He pointed as the handle slowly turned from the inside.

Nick picked up the phone as if he didn't already know who was on the other end. "Hello?"

"Ivy and Tim found Moe, so we can end this thing."

Nick smiled, enjoying the desperation in the man's voice.

"Listen, your boss wanted his stuff back and now you know where it is, so there's no reason to hurt anyone, right?"

"My boss wanted to thank you for the information and to release you from your obligation, Mr. Luzan."

The man's voice edged up an octave. "Fine, fine. I don't care about me. I want you to promise you're not going to hurt Ivy and Tim, or Moe either."

"That's a little melodramatic."

"I don't think so after what happened to Cyril and Roger Smalley."

"I did hear something about his car exploding. Tragic, really. You'd expect better from a European machine."

"Don't play games. You won't hurt them, right? You'll get your stuff back and leave them alone?"

"Goodbye, Mr. Luzan. Don't call here again."

After a nod from his boss, he disconnected and he went downstairs to hang the Closed sign in the bookstore window.

TWENTY-FOUR

Ivy stood with her hand frozen in the air as the door slowly opened. Moe peeked out, his gaze darting back and forth, mouth twitching. It took all her self-control not to shout with joy. "Moe, hi. We are so glad to see you. Are you okay?"

He nodded.

"Can we come in for a minute?"

Moe stayed motionless for a moment and then he pulled the door open.

They went in. The space was dusty and hot; the only decoration was Moe's red sleeping bag and two brown paper sacks. A tiny TV sat on an old desk, Moe's videotapes beside it.

Tim settled himself on the floor next to Moe, who had folded himself into a small ball. "Moe? Your mother has been so sad that you ran away. Can you tell us why you left?"

He rocked slowly on the grimy floor.

Ivy was pleased to see empty water bottles on the floor. The poor man was not dehydrated. A half-empty box of graham crackers sat at neat right angles to the edge of Moe's sleeping bag. She joined them. "Did you get scared?"

He stopped rocking and nodded.

"Was it because of Cyril?"

Moe nodded again.

Ivy tried to catch his eye. "Did he give you something to hold for him?"

No answer.

Tim held up a cautioning hand to Ivy before he turned back to Moe. "It must have made you very sad, when you heard Cyril died."

Moe didn't answer but his sniffles told them he'd started to cry.

Tim touched Moe gently on the arm. "It's sad when someone dies, isn't it? Your mother said you had a cat named Comet. Remember Comet?" He waited for Moe's nod. "Comet died and that made you very sad, too. Your mom said the pastor came to talk to you and he told you Comet was with Jesus."

Moe stopped rocking and put his head on his knee, eyes closed.

Tim's voice was soft. "Jesus loves all of His people just like He loves Comet."

The face Moe turned to Tim was dirty and streaked with tears. "Cyril?"

"Jesus holds Cyril next to His heart, Moe. He loves him and He loves you. When people go to live with Him, there are no more hurts or bad feelings. Do you understand?"

Ivy watched Tim as Moe wiped his sleeve across his face. At that moment, she felt an all-encompassing love for Tim. She knew, without question, that he was meant to be her soul mate, more important than her job, closer than her work brothers. The truth could not be denied any longer, no matter what the risk or the potential for hurt. Tears started up in her eyes. Tim had always been there for her. Why hadn't she seen it until now? She'd been blinded by Antonio's allure.

Swallowing hard, she fought for control. Though she wanted to wrap him in the biggest hug she could imagine and never let him go, she knew their main goal at the moment had to be solving the puzzle Cyril had left behind.

Tim had given Moe some graham crackers and a drink of water.

Ivy waited for him to eat a little. "Cyril gave you something, something to hold for him, didn't he?"

Moe nodded.

She kept her voice level. "Do you have it here with you?"

He rose and picked up the paper bag, handing it to Ivy before he went to work on the crackers again.

Hardly daring to breathe, Ivy opened the bag. It held two books. She pulled them out and laid them on the floor. One was a copy of *Animal Farm* and the other, *Cannery Row.* Her mind struggled to make sense of it. "Books?"

Tim came next to her and they flipped through the pages.

Moe's voice startled them both. "Forty-seven, six, fifteen, sixteen, seventeen."

"What does that mean, Moe?" Ivy asked.

"Forty-seven, six, fifteen, sixteen, seventeen," he repeated.

Tim flipped through *Animal Farm* and she did the same with *Cannery Row.*

"Try page forty-seven," Tim said, feverishly turning pages.

She found the page. "I don't see anything weird." Her breath caught. "Wait, wait a minute. There are some numbers stuck here in the sixth paragraph."

Tim peered over her shoulder. "Yup, just like Moe said. Page forty-seven, paragraph six, lines fifteen, sixteen and seventeen." He squinted. "If you look at every second character of those lines I'd say we've got some kind of formula, or at least part of one."

Her nerves jangled. "A formula for ZTR7 by any chance?"

He stared at her. "I'd bet money on it. And I'll bet *Animal Farm* has an interesting page or two also."

"So someone is smuggling the drug formulas…"

"Supplied by Roger Smalley…"

"…hidden in books, and Cyril found out somehow and snitched a few copies. I'll bet he did it when he worked for the package and mailing company." Ivy gaped.

"Boy did he pick the wrong package to pilfer."

She felt like she'd been trapped in a spy movie. "But who…?"

Tim removed a bookmark from between two pages. His face was grim. "It says Corner Street Bookstore, Sergei Evans proprietor."

She was struck dumb. Sergei Evans, quiet Mr. Evans, a smuggler? A murderer?

Tim's eyes danced in thought. "It's ingenious, really. Send a shipment of books to your buyer and who is going to be suspicious? Even if the books are seized by someone, who is going to take the time to go through each page to look for incriminating info? Who would think of it in the first place?"

Ivy took out her cell phone to call the police. There was no signal. "We'd better get Moe out of here and get these books to Detective Greenly."

Tim was already working, rolling Moe's sleeping bag up and talking softly to him. "We're going to get you home, Moe. Your mother will be so happy to see you. Are you ready to go?"

Moe didn't answer. He stood and packed the empty water bottles neatly into a paper bag.

Ivy put the books in her backpack.

Nick watched from his parking place just behind Tim's truck. Through his binoculars he could see them enter the cabin. He also noted the scooter parked in front of the place. Bingo.

He'd taken the time to finalize the solution with Sergei before he'd left.

"The affair has ended badly. Leave the merchandise. Just clean it up. We'll go home for a while," Evans had said.

"It's not good business. They'll look into the deaths of three people, especially a firefighter."

"It can't be helped. They may have put the details together. It would be incomplete to let them live."

"The bodies are piling up."

"You will make it look like an accident, an unforeseeable tragedy. Remove the people and the merchandise at one time."

"What about the flyboy nurse?"

"If you do your job right, there will be no evidence to support any claims he makes. Besides, the New York people will take care of him soon enough. I will arrange to borrow a large sum of money in his name. When he defaults, they will not be happy."

"You're sure?"

"Yes. We will fly home tonight on a red-eye."

Nick sighed, squelching a sliver of discomfort. It wasn't the killing that bothered him, rather the numbers. One body can be overlooked, maybe even two, but this was over the top. Still, orders were orders and he was not one to question. He held up a hand to double-check the wind. They wouldn't escape in this terrain. Death by wildfire. It was too perfect.

Then he pulled the propane torch from the trunk and fired it up, staring at the flame that flared to life, blue as the wing of a butterfly.

Ivy stiffened as the familiar smell hit her.

Smoke.

She raced outside and grabbed the binoculars. She didn't need them to see the smoke that billowed from the canyon just above their location. Through the viewer she spotted the car on the ridgeline pull out and move away. Even as she watched in horror, the flames roared to life in a wall that traveled down the narrow canyon with an audible whoosh.

The hideous facts unrolled themselves in her mind.

Wildfire was quick and deadly, and all the conditions were perfect for an inferno.

Capricious winds that could change direction in a moment.

Low humidity.

Low fuel moisture.

Rugged terrain, steep, inaccessible, heavy brush.

They'd need air tankers, strike teams, a massive response.

But there was no time. No time.

She yelled to Tim and Moe. "Someone set a fire. We've got to move now."

Tim came out, holding Moe by the hand.

"Can you get a signal on your cell phone?" Ivy asked as she pulled on her backpack.

He shook his head. "No, I tried a minute ago."

"Doesn't matter anyway. They'd never get here fast enough. The wind is funneling the fire down the canyon and everything is dry as tinder. Our only chance is to get to the truck first." She grabbed Moe's other hand and they ran, stumbling, through an ever-thickening layer of smoke.

There was no way to get around it. They were at the bottom of a canyon bordered on both sides by thickly wooded mountains. The woods, she knew, were severely desiccated thanks to the unusually dry spring. The dry pines would burn like napalm on a stick. She'd seen them literally explode from the ferocious heat.

Moe stumbled and fell. He lay in a ball, whimpering. Tim knelt next to him. "It's okay, Moe. We've got to run to the truck and we'll be okay."

Ivy dared a look around. She saw a thick wall of flame moving behind them, engulfing everything in its wake. The crowns of the trees glowed like embers, and Ivy knew the fire would jump from tree to tree like a live thing. In spite of her training, her years of fighting fire, she felt the fear take hold in her gut. Being burned alive, what a way to go.

Shoving an arm under Moe's elbow, with Tim on the other side, she propelled him along. "We've got to run."

She thought about trying to make it to the river that ran along the west side of the canyon, but it was rough ground, boulder-strewn and thick with grass. The best option, the only option, was to get to the truck.

They half carried Moe, tripping and faltering as they raced over the dry grass. She fell heavily, feeling a snap as her wrist gave under her. Tim was there, helping her up.

"Are you hurt?"

She gritted her teeth. "I think I broke my wrist."

No time to think about the injury. She could hear it now, the crackle and hiss of the fire bearing down on them. The truck came into view, gleaming white against the blackness.

"Only a little farther," she yelled over the din. "Keep running."

Her blood surged as they reached the truck. Tim fumbled for the keys, jamming them into the door.

Moe tugged on Ivy's arm.

"It's okay, we're going to make it Moe," she said as calmly as she could, coughing against the acrid fumes.

He tugged again.

When she finally looked at the spot where he pointed, her knees almost gave way.

The tires, all four of them, were flat, slashed by the fire setter's knife.

TWENTY-FIVE

"**Y**ou've got to take me, Charlie. There's a reason you own your own helicopter and now is the time to put it to use."

Charlie blinked, staring at him. "Mitch, what are you saying? Somebody is going to kill Ivy and Tim? How? Why?"

"I can't explain it now. We've got to get to Sugar Pine Lodge." He unrolled a map on the table. "Here. You've got to fly me here."

"That's crazy. We can't just take off at the drop of a hat. There are procedures."

Mitch slammed his hands down on the table. "Listen, Charlie. I've messed up, screwed up my life with gambling and ruined my future. Please help me before they pay the price for my sins. I'm begging you."

Charlie let out a deep breath and nodded. "Okay. Let's do it."

They drove at breakneck speed to the private airstrip where Charlie kept his chopper. Ignoring the strange look from a mechanic working on a small plane, they jumped in and buckled up.

Charlie flipped on the radio to catch any emergency traffic.

Moving rapidly away from the airstrip, Charlie and Mitch exchanged an agonized look when a message came over the radio.

Wildfire.

North side of Sugar Pine Mountain.

Code three response required from all available personnel.

Mitch swallowed hard. "Please, God," he whispered. "Don't let me be too late."

* * *

Ivy stared at the tires. A strange calm settled over her. They were trapped. There was no possible way to outrun the fire without the truck. No options, no way out.

Entrapment was a firefighter's worst nightmare, but she didn't feel afraid for herself. Instead she looked over at the two men who both watched her with a look of horror on their faces.

The fire was close now, so close she could feel the heat warming her neck.

Tim understood. She could see it in his face.

"We're out of options," he said, his voice steady.

She nodded.

He looked at her, his eyes bright, a love and longing in his face that took her breath away. Then he inhaled deeply and turned to Moe. He took his hand and turned him away from the fire. "We'll watch this way now, Moe. I see a lot of pinecones. Do you want to help me count them?"

Her heart fractured into tiny pieces. Tim, spending his last minutes trying to ease the soul of another. It had taken her so very long to realize what he meant to her. She loved him. For the first time, it felt completely right. And now she would lose it all in a matter of minutes.

She felt an exquisite shiver go through her like a rush of cold water. A determination took hold and filled her mind and senses. The decision came in an instant. She would not give him up, give them up, until every last bit of life was burned out of her body.

She felt around on the bottom of her backpack with her good hand.

They were still there, two fire shelters, the thin film of aluminum that had saved some lives in desperate circumstances.

Some lives.

She removed them and Sergei's doctored books, which she stuffed into her waistband before she dropped to the ground.

Tim saw her movement out of the corner of his eye. He turned to watch her scooping pine needles and leaves away until she'd cleared a small circle, fumbling because of her injured wrist.

Tim fell to his knees, copying her. "What are we doing?"

"Clearing the ground of any fuels. We're going to use the fire shelters."

He didn't answer, didn't question. It was the only way. God willing, they could make it work, they would make it work.

He pushed her gently to the side and began to scrape away the debris until the area was as clear as he could make it, until his fingers were raw and bloody.

They had to yell now, to be heard over the advancing fire. "I've only got two shelters and they're made to protect one," Ivy yelled. "I'm going to put Moe in mine with me. Watch how I do it so you can deploy the other one."

"No way," he yelled back. "Moe is going in mine."

"This isn't the time to argue. They're not designed for two. You take the single."

Blood roared in his ears. He grabbed her by the arms and shouted so loud his voice crested the noise of the fire. "You listen to me. Forget your hero stuff, forget your constant need to be in charge, forget it all. You are going to have the best chance I can give you to survive, do you hear me? I will not risk your life any more than we have to." His voice dropped slightly. "I am not going to tell your mother that she's lost another daughter to fire. Moe is with me and that's the end of the story. Am I making myself very clear, Ivy?"

She blinked, mouth open. "You don't even know how to deploy one," she yelled.

He let her go. "I can follow directions. Anybody can be a hero, Ivy." For a moment, he thought she would not acquiesce. Then without a word she handed him the shelter and a pair of gloves.

"Watch. We only have another minute. When you get in, put on the gloves and hold the shelter in place, keep your face as close to the ground as you can." She tried to pull the red ring to split the plastic down the middle, but the bundle slipped out of her numb hand.

He took it from her, opened hers and helped her position it around herself. When he was sure she had her bag in place, he unfurled the long silver strip on the other one. They hooked their feet under the straps and grabbed the top straps with their hands.

"Okay. Put Moe underneath you so he doesn't move. Fold down the floor panels and hold them down under your legs. Push the sides away from your body to make a space for air."

Tim nodded as he fumbled with the fabric, energy pulsing through him like an electric current. "If I remember correctly, this will buy us only a few minutes."

Her eyes were wide. "Don't come out until you're absolutely sure the fire has passed over."

He nodded, a tension filling every pore, every atom of his being. "All right, then. Let's do it."

Tim talked quietly to Moe. Somehow he got the man to come and they crawled into the shelter. The fire was nearly upon them. He felt the heat, the angry exhalation of the fire as it chewed up the final distance between them. He watched her face, just before she disappeared into the shelter. He saw it all there in her eyes—the love, the fear, the faith.

"God," he whispered, "if You can't save all of us, please save her. Save Ivy."

He tucked himself inside and the fire was upon them.

Mitch strained to see through the smoke.

"These conditions aren't safe," Charlie yelled over the roar of the rotor. "We've got to pull out. They're going to bring in an air tanker soon and we can't be in the way."

"One more minute." He stiffened in shock, leaning against the small window. "I can see them. They're deploying shelters. We're too late." He watched in despair as the fire swallowed them up.

Ivy's brain reminded her that the air was a few precious degrees cooler at ground level. She knew the material was designed to withstand temperatures of up to four hundred degrees. She also knew that conditions outside the shelter would kill her instantly. Still, the overwhelming panic that filled her every cell took all her strength to combat.

As the shelter began to shudder from the fire-generated winds, she started to pray.

The heat became unbearable. Where the wind pressed the shelter sides into her body, her skin burned.

Through the pinholes in the fabric she could see firelight like living embers devouring the very space in which she lay.

"Please, Lord."

The scream of the fire, with all the power of a monster, bore down on her, buffeting the shelter, trying to rip it from her hands.

"Save us," she screamed in her mind as her body seemed to boil from the excruciating heat.

Mitch and Charlie watched as the flames passed over the shelter and traveled in increasing fury down the canyon.

"Did they…?" Charlie started again. "Do you think they made it?"

"Put her down there." Mitch pointed to a charred spot away from the shelters.

"That fire can change direction in a second. I'll keep her running. You go check. We've only got minutes, Mitch, I mean it. Minutes."

He eased the helicopter toward the ravaged ground.

It took an agonizing period of time for the roar to recede, the scorching air to cool slightly, ever so slightly. She forced herself to wait, wait, wait. One breath of hot, toxic gases would suffocate her in less than a minute. She yelled as loud as she could. "Tim, Moe. Can you hear me?"

There was no answer from the other shelter.

Her fear turned to a live thing, crawling through her body until she could not stand it. She fought her way out of the shelter, burning her arm on the still-hot material. On hands and knees, she crawled to the shelter, avoiding the patches of smoking ground.

"Tim. Answer me, please."

Only two feet left until she would reach him. What would she find? She was too terrified even to offer up a prayer.

"Tim. Please."

Mitch dove from the chopper. He ran, trying not to breathe in the noxious fumes. There was movement ahead from one of the shelters. The other was still, deathly still.

Ivy reached out a trembling hand.

The shelter opened and Tim's pale face emerged, Moe peeking around his shoulder.

She threw herself at him, holding on to him for all he was worth. She pressed her lips to his, the acrid taste of fire on both their mouths. "Oh, Tim, I thought I'd lost you. I couldn't bear it."

He smoothed her sweaty hair from her face. "I couldn't either. But we made it."

Ivy made sure Moe was all right. Though he was trembling and his hand was badly burned, he had escaped relatively unscathed. She half cried, half laughed as she looked at them both, sooty and smelling of smoke. "Thank you, God," she breathed. "I've never been so scared in my whole life."

Tim gave her a haughty look. "I told you I could follow directions."

With a heart overflowing with joy, she wrapped her arms around him again.

Ivy was startled when Mitch ran up to them. In the terror and excitement she hadn't caught site of Charlie's helicopter. Mitch grabbed her in a fierce hug.

"Oh, thank God for saving you, thank God." He squeezed her so hard her burned back made her gasp in pain.

He pulled her to arm's length. "You're hurt?"

"Not badly, my wrist and Moe's hand is burned. How did you find us?"

"Never mind that now. Let's get out of here."

Ivy heard the distant wail of sirens. She knew they would be bringing in mutual aid from the neighboring counties to combat the ferocious fire. Though she felt a small twinge at missing the action, it was a very small one. Most of all she felt an overwhelming gratitude that God had spared their lives and an unrestrained joy that she'd finally admitted the truth to herself and to Tim.

The four of them made their way to Charlie's chopper. It was a tight fit, but they crammed inside and Charlie lifted off.

"Well, now," he yelled over the engine. "You folks had us a mite worried there. I've only known a few folks who deployed their shelters."

And lived, Ivy thought grimly. "Thanks for picking us up."

"Thank Mitch. He practically commandeered my bird."

Ivy tried to ask Mitch again how he'd found them, but he waved her off, focusing instead on tending to Moe's hand with his first-aid kit. Charlie flew them back to the airstrip and drove them to the hospital. On the way, Ivy phoned Madge while Moe and Charlie counted the various buttons and knobs on the car's dashboard.

She had to hold the cell away from her ear to manage Madge's piercing shrieks of joy. She promised, amid much crying, to meet them at the hospital. Ivy disconnected. "She's overwhelmed."

"So I heard," Tim said, putting a hand on her good wrist and lowering his voice so only she could hear. "And so am I. Did you mean it? What you said back there?"

His face was so vulnerable, so childlike. "I did. I realized what it would be like to lose you for good."

Tim sighed. "I felt the same way."

Charlie called over his shoulder. "So Mitch isn't telling me anything. Who set the fire up there?"

"Oh, gosh," Ivy said. "I didn't tell him." She looked guiltily at the books sitting next to her on the seat.

"You'll have a chance to real soon. He's following right behind us, but the suspense is killing me. What is going on?"

They finished the story just as Charlie pulled into the hospital parking lot. "That's quite a tale. I never would have suspected Sergei in a million years."

"Me, neither."

Ivy had an idea. "Charlie, can you take these books over to the police station right now? The sooner they have the info, the safer we'll all be."

He agreed and they parted company.

Mitch hurried into the emergency room on the heels of a sobbing Madge. She folded Moe into an enormous hug and rocked them both back and forth. A nurse waited until they were through and escorted them both back to tend to Moe's injuries.

Tim and Ivy exchanged a satisfied look.

Mitch shook his head. "I can't believe how close you were to not making it."

Tim waved in a dismissive gesture. "We had it all under control. Right, Ivy?"

She laughed. "I'm so glad you felt that way. As for me, I had a doubt or two there for a minute." She looked at Mitch, who did not share their smile. "What's wrong, Mitch?"

He closed his eyes for a minute. "You go get yourself taken care of and I'll explain it all when you're done."

She hesitated.

"Go on," he said. "Please. Get those burns seen to. And your wrist."

Ivy did, though her treatment was interrupted by a call from Jeff. The nurse handed her a phone and she listened to him yelling over the siren noise. "I heard you deployed the Shake 'n' Bake. I can't believe it. Are you all right? Tim and Moe, too?"

"Yes, believe it or not, I'm okay. Some minor burns, but all three of us are fine. Are you en route?"

"Yeah. Me and everyone else in the county. Some fire."

"Yeah, some fire. Be careful. The winds are tricky."

"Will do and when you come back you can give us the first-hand account of your experience."

"I'd be happy to. Bye, Jeff."

She clicked off and the doctor finished disinfecting and bandaging the burns on her back and shins. They splinted her wrist after she promised to return later for an X-ray. She still felt the elation of their escape; the joy of her love for Tim but worry about Mitch pushed her to hurry out to the waiting room.

Tim was there waiting. Mitch was gone.

"Where is he? I'm worried."

"So am I." Tim handed her an envelope. "He left this for you."

TWENTY-SIX

She read the letter aloud.

Hey, V,

I really screwed up this time. Sergei Evans had a few deals going besides selling books. He called and offered me a loan in exchange for info about you. And I believed him. Stupid, huh? But then I've been making a lot of bonehead choices lately.

He promised he just wanted to keep tabs on you until you found Moe, said Moe had something of his. Ivy, I promise, I never thought he would hurt you or Moe. I figured Cyril probably got himself into some trouble with the people he stole from and they whacked him. I didn't even suspect Sergei had him killed, but after Smalley bought the farm I couldn't deny it anymore. I figured if I could get to Moe first, get whatever he had and return it to Evans, the whole mess would be over.

When I finally realized what kind of man Sergei was, it was too late and you and Tim and Moe almost got killed. It was all my fault. I hope you'll be able to forgive me someday.

I got the books from Charlie before he gave them to the cops. I had to punch him and when he comes to, he's going to kill me if Evans doesn't first. Anyway, I'm going to give Evans his books and end this thing.

I'm sorry, V. I love you.
Mitch

Ivy's pulse pounded in terror. "He's going to the bookstore. We've got to stop him."

Tim hastily arranged to borrow Madge's car and they sped toward the bookstore. Ivy realized she'd lost her cell phone somewhere in their wild escape. The only thing left clipped to her waistband was the radio pager. "Did you keep your phone by any chance?"

He gave her a sheepish look as he handed her the phone. "I know you told me to throw away all the equipment that I had on me when we got into the shelter, but I was preoccupied trying to get Moe to settle down."

"How did you get him into that shelter, anyway?"

"I set him to work counting the creases from where the thing was folded."

"I didn't even notice any creases," she said as she dialed.

"I didn't either at first, but it kept him from running away."

She got through to Greenly as they pulled up in front of the bookstore.

"I'm already on my way. There's a really angry pilot in my office who told me an incredible story. Don't go in there, do you hear me? My people will be there in minutes."

"Hurry." She hung up.

The bookstore windows were shuttered, the Closed sign hanging in the front window. They got out, keeping behind the shelter of the car. Ivy noticed for the first time how dirty and singed she and Tim both looked. A lock of hair on the back of his head was blackened at the tip. An anger swelled inside her. The idea that someone, anyone, would use fire to kill people, a fire that could wipe out thousands of acres and hundreds of homes, made her furious.

"I can't believe Evans is so two-faced," she whispered.

"Yeah. He seemed like such a stand-up guy."

They both jumped when something crashed into the upstairs window.

"Did you see what I saw?"

Tim nodded slowly. "That sure looked like a man's body to me."

"And he had dark hair." Fear mixed with the anger. "Just like Mitch."

Evans picked up the books from the floor.

"Thank you, Nick. He was becoming out of control."

Nick nodded, looked at the crumpled figure on the floor. "They always think there's a free lunch. Shame."

"We'll have to leave right now." Evans sighed. "This cannot be salvaged. I will tidy up here while you bring the car around."

Nick headed down the narrow stairs.

They found the back door open, a new sedan parked out back. Tim crept around the car while Ivy peeked in the window. No sign of movement. No sign of Mitch.

Tim rejoined her. "This is a bad idea, Ivy. We should wait for the cops."

"I know, but Mitch may be hurt in there, dying even. I'll understand if you'd rather wait out here."

He arched an eyebrow. "Yeah, like that's going to happen. Let's move."

Nick heard the sound of the door opening. He stopped to listen. One, two people. Not cops, there was no squeak of leather or jangle of metal. Ah, it was the firefighter and her friend. He smiled. Strong stamina to escape that fire, like the Chinook salmon he'd caught last year that fought with its last ounce of life. Inspiring, really. He unsheathed the knife from his belt and eased down the stairs.

Ivy bent low, winding her way through the stacks toward the place where the steps led to the upstairs. Tim headed the other direction, to open the front door for the cops. Though her burned shins complained with every step, she forced herself to go slow, peeking around each shelf, inching her way forward.

A pair of luminous eyes made her gasp. It was an owl, stuffed, glaring at her from a spot on a high shelf. She steadied her breathing and continued forward until she heard it. From her left, the sound of voices.

Tim's words echoed in the quiet of the store. "The police are on their way."

She crept forward on hands and knees until she neared the cash register. Peeking around a pile of boxes, she saw Tim, standing with his back to her, and facing him was the big blond man holding a knife.

The man had a slight smile on his face. "You have remarkable determination, to outlive that fire."

"And you have no moral compass to set it in the first place." Tim's hands were raised slightly in front of him, as though he was preparing to ward off the stab of the knife.

Ivy's mind wheeled. He was going to kill Tim, and Ivy knew without a doubt that he would do it with no qualms at all. What could she do? Her radio pager chafed against her waist as she shifted slightly.

"It will have to do," she said silently as she unclipped it. Praying her shoulder would hold out, she lobbed the thing as hard as she could over the top of a nearby book stack. It clattered down with a loud crash.

The pale man looked up for a split second and Tim launched himself like a spring. He locked hands around the knife and they went down in a pile of arms and legs. Ivy dashed over, watching in horror as the knife flashed and danced between them. She grabbed the man's foot and twisted hard. She heard the clank of the knife coming loose and hitting the floor.

A vicious kick sent her sprawling backward, smashing into the wooden bookcase. It took a moment for her to blink away the flashes of light that danced across her vision.

She heard Tim grunt in pain. "Tim? Tim, are you all right?"

There was no answer. She had to get to Tim.

Then the big man was standing above her, hands fisted on his hips, light hair eerie in the dimness.

"You have taken a very long time to die," he said.

She tried to sit up, her head still filled with sparkles of light. "I never was very good at going along with the program."

A loud thwack sounded above her and the man fell to his knees, a bemused look on his face before he pitched face downward to the floor. Tim came into view, holding the enormous book he'd wielded.

He wiped a smear of blood from his cheek and patted the heavy volume. "My mother always told me to keep a dictionary handy."

Tim reached down a hand to Ivy.

Without warning, Sergei was there, appearing out of nowhere around a bookshelf. He leveled a gun at Ivy and sighed. "I do apologize, but I'm afraid I will have to kill you both."

Ivy sat up. "You must be some kind of monster."

He blinked. "No, not a monster. Just a determined business-man who doesn't allow distractions."

Tim took a step closer. "Not distractions. People. People like Cyril whom you killed and people like Moe who would have died if we hadn't interfered."

Sergei's eyes flicked to his watch. "I've not the time for dramatics, I'm afraid."

"The cops will be here any minute," Ivy said desperately.

He smiled. "Then I will make this quick."

Sergei did not finish the last syllable before Tim hurled himself at the gun. It went off with a thunderous clap, tearing a chunk out of the bookshelf next to her head.

Ivy tried to scramble to her feet, but her wrist gave out and she fell back to the floor. Terror gripped her insides as she watched the man she loved strain to get the upper hand.

Sweat poured off Tim's face, his mouth twisted into a grimace.

The gun fired again, a bullet whizzing over their heads and exploding a lamp into a shower of glass shards. She heard the sound of a siren above the noise.

The men thrashed across the floor but Tim's strength and youth won out. With a powerful twist he knocked the gun from Sergei's hand and rolled the man onto his stomach. Ivy thought the fight was over when Sergei leveled a kick that caught Tim in the stomach. Sergei scrambled to his feet and ran out the door.

Still half doubled over, Tim looked at her, panting and bleeding from a cut above his eyebrow. "You okay?"

She nodded slowly, tears starting in her eyes. "As long as you are."

A feeling swelled inside her and broke through the walls of hesitation and fear. It moved like a mighty wind through her soul and propelled her to her feet. She couldn't wait one second longer. She threw herself into his arms. "I love you, Tim. I love you so much."

He was quiet for a moment, his face buried in her hair. When he answered, his voice was hoarse. "I feel like I've been waiting a lifetime to hear you say that." He lifted his head and put his hands on either side of her face. "I've never loved anyone as much as I love you. I've prayed for so long, so long to see that look in your eyes."

His lips were soft against hers, molding her mouth in a kiss that told her everything.

Ivy smiled through her tears. "I can't believe it's taken me so long to figure it out. You've been there for me through all the ups and downs."

He pressed feather kisses to her cheeks and brow. "It doesn't matter. You love me and that's good enough to last me for a lifetime."

She sighed, a deeply peaceful feeling filling her chest, momentarily overriding her concern for Mitch, her fear of their attackers. For that one precious moment, the truth of her feelings had set her free, set them both free.

Detective Greenly and two other officers barreled in the door, guns drawn. One headed upstairs.

Greenly looked at them in amazement. "I don't know what to say about you two."

Tim kept his arm around Ivy. "Where's Sergei?"

"We got him trying to start his car. It seems someone ripped out the ignition wires."

"Really?" Tim clucked. "This neighborhood is definitely going to the dogs."

Ivy's fear returned. "My cousin. Where is he?"

An officer's voice called from upstairs. "Got a guy up here. He's alive. Unconscious from a good crack on the head."

Ivy sighed in relief. He was alive. Mitch was alive. Maybe, with Detective Greenly's help, they could get him out of the mess he'd gotten himself into.

Together Ivy and Tim walked outside, watching as an ambulance crew arrived to treat Mitch. Tim put an arm around her. "That was some overhand pitch. Looks like the shoulder is getting back up to snuff."

"Uh-huh. I'm going to be back on the line soon. I can feel it."

He nodded, a wistful look coming over his face. "You got a nasty bump. Do you have any blurred vision?"

She looked up into his face and placed a hand gently on his cheek. "No, I think for the first time in my life I can see everything perfectly clearly." She pulled his face to hers and kissed him.

* * * * *

Dear Reader,

Ivy Beria is a hero. In her professional capacity she saves lives,
protects property and holds a place in a tightly knit firefighter
family. One moment too long in a burning house and Ivy is sep-
arated from her job and the status that comes with it. She's cut
off from the brotherhood, and forced to face her own anger at
losing her sister so many years ago.

Tim Carnelli has been in love with Ivy for years, but she's
never given him a chance. He's not a firefighter, and what's
more, he's devoted to the same God Ivy believes took her sister
away in a horrific accident. When circumstances conspire to put
her neighbor Moe, an autistic savant, in harm's way, Ivy sets
aside her pride and teams up with Tim to keep Moe safe.

This book explores the identities we forge for ourselves, identities that can pull our attention away from our life in Him. Can
there be heroism in humility? Honor in the ordinary? Ivy strug-
gles to find the answers and to let go of the pain that separates
her from Him.

I am so pleased that you chose to read *Flashover.* It has been
my pleasure to write it. I would love to hear from you via my
Web site at www.danamentink.com.

Fondly,

Dana Mentink

QUESTIONS FOR DISCUSSION

1. What sort of qualities does it take for a woman to do a traditionally male job?

2. Ivy disobeys a direct order and stays in the burning house for what she feels are noble reasons. Was she justified in doing so? What decision would you have made in her place?

3. As a culture do we still believe that misfortune is just punishment for sin? What does the Bible say about that?

4. Mitch tends to Ivy in the helicopter after she is hurt in the structure collapse. What is your initial impression of his character?

5. Sergei Evans behaves as though he is superior to others. Is this feeling of entitlement a common one in the modern world? Is it a sin to believe that we are deserving of a certain type of treatment, good or bad? How have you dealt with people who acted as if they were entitled to everything?

6. Nick says, "Waiting was a skill, a talent so many people lacked." Do you agree or not? How can people learn to be more patient?

7. Ivy is described as Miss I Gotta Be in Charge of Everything. Do you know people who seem to fit this description? Is it a role today's women feel pressured to fill? How can we learn to let go of some things?

8. Ivy feels uncomfortable when Tim starts up his "God talk." Why do you think Ivy doesn't want to hear Tim speak about God? Have you encountered a similar attitude in people you know?

9. Ivy is not a "good relaxer." What are some techniques she could try to help her with this?

10. Why does Ivy focus on the death of her sister, rather than remembering the time they spent together?

11. Tim is not the traditional hero. His actions are quiet and self-sacrificing. As a culture we place more value on the dramatic acts of heroism than the humble actions of God-fearing people. Do you agree or disagree? Why?

12. What are some ways that people can keep from defining themselves through their occupation?

Love Inspired
HISTORICAL

*Powerful, engaging stories of romance, adventure and faith set
in the past—when things were simpler and faith played a
major role in everyday lives.*

Turn the page for a sneak preview of
THE MAVERICK PREACHER
by
Victoria Bylin

*Love Inspired Historical—love and faith
throughout the ages*

Mr. Blue looked into her eyes with silent understanding and she wondered if he, too, had struggled with God's ways. The slash of his brow looked tight with worry, and his whiskers were too stubbly to be permanent. Adie thought about his shaving tools and wondered when he'd used them last. Her new boarder would clean up well on the outside, but his heart remained a mystery. She needed to keep it that way. The less she knew about him, the better.

"Good night," she said. "Bessie will check you in the morning."

"Before you go, I've been wondering…"

"About what?"

"The baby… Who's the mother?"

Adie raised her chin. "I am."

Earlier he'd called her "Miss Clarke" and she hadn't corrected him. The flash in his eyes told her that he'd assumed she'd given birth out of wedlock. Adie resented being judged, but she counted it as the price of protecting Stephen. If Mr. Blue chose to condemn her, so be it. She'd done nothing for which to be ashamed. With their gazes locked, she waiting for the criticism that didn't come.

Instead he laced his fingers on top of the Bible. "Children are a gift, all of them."

"I think so, too."

He lightened his tone. "A boy or a girl?"

"A boy."

The man smiled. "He sure can cry. How old is he?"

Adie didn't like the questions at all, but she took pride in her son. "He's three months old." She didn't mention that he'd been born six weeks early. "I hope the crying doesn't disturb you."

"I don't care if it does."

He sounded defiant. She didn't understand. "Most men would be annoyed."

"The crying's better than silence... I know."

Adie didn't want to care about this man, but her heart fluttered against her ribs. What did Joshua Blue know of babies and silence? Had he lost a wife? A child of his own? She wanted to express sympathy but couldn't. If she pried into his life, he'd pry into hers. He'd ask questions and she'd have to hide the truth. *Stephen was born too soon and his mother died. He barely survived. I welcome his cries, every one of them. They mean he's alive.*

With a lump in her throat, she turned to leave. "Good night, Mr. Blue."

"Good night."

A thought struck her and she turned back to his room. "I suppose I should call you Reverend."

He grimaced. "I'd prefer Josh."

* * * * *

Don't miss this deeply moving Love Inspired Historical story about a man of God who's lost his way and the woman who helps him rediscover his faith—and his heart.
THE MAVERICK PREACHER
by Victoria Bylin
available February 2009.

And also look for
THE MARSHAL TAKES A BRIDE
by Renee Ryan,
in which a lawman meets his match in a feisty schoolteacher with marriage on her mind.

Love Inspired®
SUSPENSE
RIVETING INSPIRATIONAL ROMANCE

The photographs Samantha Reid uncovers in her new store could be deadly. They present new insight into a cold case someone wants to keep closed. And when Samantha is pushed into the spotlight, Ryan Davidson–sole survivor of the slain family–must intervene to keep her safe.

Look for

EVIDENCE *of* MURDER

by **JILL ELIZABETH NELSON**

Available February 2009
wherever books are sold.

Steeple
Hill®

LIS44327

Love Inspired®
SUSPENSE

TITLES AVAILABLE NEXT MONTH

Don't miss these four stories on sale
February 10, 2009

ON A KILLER'S TRAIL by Susan Page Davis
When a sweet, elderly lady is found dead
on Christmas Day, rookie reporter Kate Richards
jumps on the story. Detective Neil Alexander can't
figure out the murderer's motive, but he *does* know
that Kate needs watching. They're on a killer's trail.
And who knows what they'll find....

FRAMED! by Robin Caroll
Without a Trace
The prime suspect in her brother's murder: Max Pershing,
the man Ava Renault has always secretly loved. To help
Max, she'll have to overcome their feuding families and
expose the truth.

EVIDENCE OF MURDER by Jill Elizabeth Nelson
The photographs Samantha Reid uncovers in her new store
could be deadly. They present new insight into a cold case
someone wants to keep closed. And when Samantha is
pushed into the spotlight, Ryan Davidson—sole survivor
of the slain family—must intervene to keep her safe.

DEADLY REUNION by Florence Case
Her sister's engaged to a murderer. Police officer
Angie Delitano is convinced of it. Then Angie uncovers
startling new evidence, forcing her to turn to Boone, the
handsome, hardened lawyer she once loved. Now she
has to learn to trust him again—with the case and
with her heart.

LISCNMBPA0109